"Still trying to get

Eve sighed. "I just don'
so reluctant to work with me to solve these cases."

Heat suffused Hoge's face. "I'm sorry," he said, and hoped she recognized that he was sincere.

He stepped back to where he'd left the evidence. Eve joined him, and instead of making the space feel smaller, she somehow made it seem brighter and more open.

"We have suspects," she said. "I can run their DNA against the killer's recovered from the crime scenes."

He shook his head. "It's too dangerous."

Not only was she *in* danger but she posed a danger. To the killer... But she also posed a danger to Hoge. Ever since the mayor had hired Eve to work these cold cases, something had shifted inside him, and he felt more vulnerable now than he had in years.

Ever since **Lisa Childs** read her first romance novel (a Harlequin story, of course) at age eleven, all she wanted was to be a romance writer. With over seventy novels published with Harlequin, Lisa is living her dream. She is an award-winning, bestselling romance author. She loves to hear from readers, who can contact her on Facebook or through her website, lisachilds.com.

JUSTICE OVERDUE

LISA CHILDS

LOVE INSPIRED
INSPIRATIONAL ROMANCE

LOVE INSPIRED®
INSPIRATIONAL ROMANCE

Recycling programs
for this product may
not exist in your area.

ISBN-13: 978-1-335-63341-5

Justice Overdue

Copyright © 2021 by Lisa Childs

This edition published by arrangement with Harlequin Books S.A.

For questions and comments about the quality of this book, please contact us at CustomerService@Harlequin.com.

Love Inspired
22 Adelaide St. West, 40th Floor
Toronto, Ontario M5H 4E3, Canada
www.LoveInspired.com

Printed in U.S.A.

He loveth righteousness and judgment:
the earth is full of the goodness of the Lord.
—*Psalm* 33:5

With great appreciation for my many blessings—
my loving, supportive husband, Andrew,
and our amazing kids!

Chapter One

"You're going to regret ordering me here," Sheriff Hogan Moore murmured to himself as he pulled his SUV into the parking lot of city hall. The white brick building was positioned prominently in the center of the town square of Cold Creek, Michigan.

Hoge had rolled down the window, but the SUV still reeked of bug spray and perspiration, like Hoge. As he turned off the ignition, he glanced into the rearview mirror and hardly recognized the man who stared back at him. His dark hair had grown overly long and bushy like the beard covering his face. After eleven days in the woods, he needed a shave, a haircut and a shower—desperately.

But this mayoral summons had cut his two-week vacation a few days short and brought him directly to city hall. Hoge pushed open the driver's-side door and stepped onto the asphalt. He tipped his head back and, despite his sunglasses, squinted up at the bright sky and murmured, "God, please grant me patience..."

Then at least one of them would have it.

The mayor clearly did not.

Mud trailing from his hiking boots, he headed across the lot to the sidewalk and up the wide redbrick steps to the front door of city hall. Cold Creek was a small town and relatively—or at least recently—safe, but a gray-haired security guard stood inside the foyer. Not that Bob Dempski provided all that much security. The retired sheriff's deputy generally just waved everyone through.

But he stopped Hoge to ask, "Catch anything?"

Hoge grinned and stretched his arms out wide.

Bob chuckled. "Trying to make me more jealous than I already am?"

"You should have taken the time off," he said. Hoge was glad that he had; he'd needed it to recharge, refocus and remind himself what mattered most.

All God's gifts.

Nature. The woods in early fall with the leaves just beginning to change color was a beautiful sight that Hoge would never fail to appreciate, like the crisp clear water of Cold Creek—which was really more river than stream.

Friends. Not everyone he'd invited to join him at the cabin had been able to, but Ted had taken some time off from his busy career to spend with him. *Uncle* Ted…

Family. Ted had been Hoge's father's friend for so long that he'd become Hoge's honorary uncle, his godfather. Being with Uncle Ted made Hoge feel close to Pop, too, despite it being a couple of years since his dad had died.

"Next time," Bob promised wistfully.

Hoge nodded. "Good."

Bob was another old friend of his father's, but then everyone had been Rolland Moore's friend, even most of the criminals he'd arrested during the long time he'd served as sheriff of Cold Creek. His dad had been such a good man. If only Hoge could be half the man his father was…

"Weren't you supposed to be off for two weeks?" Bob asked, his brow creasing beneath a lock of iron gray hair.

Hoge sighed. "Yup…"

Bob's face flushed and he chuckled. "Prentice called you in early, eh?"

Hoge nodded. "And he's probably pacing his office wondering what's taking me so long to get here."

Bob chuckled. "If he'd ever gone up to the cabin with your dad, he'd realize that the roads are more two-track trails than streets."

"He always turned down Pop's invitations," he reminded Bob. His father had included everyone on his fishing trips, figuring the more the merrier.

"Maybe you should invite him," Bob suggested.

Hoge shrugged off the suggestion. He wasn't like his father; he knew that more wasn't always merrier but usually more stressful. He wouldn't be inviting the mayor along on his fishing trips. Not that Paul Prentice would have ever accepted his invitation if he'd made it.

"I better get to his office." He didn't wait for the elevator to bring him to the third floor. Instead he hurried up the elaborate interior stairwell, his boots dropping traces of mud on each marble tread.

He winced with regret that somebody would have to clean up after him. If only Paul had listened to him, but the man had been insistent that Hoge come straight to city hall.

The third-floor landing opened up to a reception area

with a couple of executive assistants sharing the large space. One worked for the deputy mayor, while the other worked for the mayor—he walked over to that desk.

Alice, with her pretty white hair, had worked in city hall for a long time. She greeted Hoge with a smile and a chuckle. "You are so very much like your father."

He sucked in a breath. If only that were true…

"Rolland loved to fish, too," Alice said. "Too bad you had to cut your trip short."

Hoge leaned closer to her desk and asked, "Do you know why?"

Her face flushed a bit, so she knew. But she was loyal enough to the mayor that she refrained from saying anything more than, "He's waiting in his office."

With a sigh, Hoge headed toward the door to the suite of offices Paul had converted into one large space. It had been his first act once he'd been sworn in to office during his first term six years ago. When Hoge closed his hand over the knob, Alice called out a warning. "He's not alone."

Was this an ambush of some sort? Ever since Hoge had been elected sheriff two years ago, the mayor had been testing him. He wasn't the only one, though. Other people tested Hoge, too, to see if he was as good as his father. Prentice tried to see if Hoge could be manipulated. Rolland Moore had always made it clear that he worked *with* the mayor— not for him. Hoge needed to get that message across, as well.

But how?

Not by cutting his vacation short at Prentice's request…

But the mayor had told him that it was important. Really important.

If it wasn't…

He would desperately need that patience for which he'd prayed in the parking lot. He drew in a deep breath, bracing himself, and then he opened the door.

The mayor paused as if in midpace around his mammoth office and glanced at the open door. Paul Prentice was a little younger than Hoge's father, who would have turned sixty-three this year. But with his golden hair, deep tan and impeccable wardrobe, Prentice looked even younger than he really was. Paul's mouth twisted into a grimace of distaste, likely at the unkempt sight of Hoge. "Sheriff—"

His mouth twitching with the temptation to grin, Hoge reminded the mayor, "I warned you that I should stop home first, but you wanted me to come straight here. What's so important that you demanded I finish my vacation early?"

The mayor stepped aside then, revealing a visitor sitting in one of two leather chairs in front of his desk. Hoge had been told that the mayor wasn't alone, but he was still caught off guard. The female visitor was young and pretty and somehow vaguely familiar.

He narrowed his eyes behind his sunglasses, which he still needed due to the sunlight streaming through the tall windows, and studied her delicately featured face. She reached up and pushed up her glasses, a pair of black-rimmed ones that slid back down her small nose. Her blond hair was pulled up on top of her head, and she wore a suit that was nearly the same blue of her eyes.

She was really pretty.

She stood up and crossed the room, holding out her hand toward him. The click of her heels against the highly polished hardwood floors Paul had had installed echoed throughout the space. "I'm Eve Collins," she said.

He closed his hand around hers and shook it gently before releasing it. Her nose wrinkled, and probably not just to hold up her glasses but from the stench of him. He really needed to shower.

"Sorry for my appearance," he apologized. "I've been up at my cabin for several days."

She arched one blond brow. "And there's no running water?"

He shook his head. "Nope. It's really primitive." And he loved how it always brought him back to the basics, back to what was important. Nature. Friends. Family.

"I figured you'd be in church yesterday," the mayor remarked to Hoge. "So I didn't think you'd be coming straight from the cabin."

Hoge didn't like to miss a service, but there was another kind of church out in the woods, by the creek…a sense of spirituality more profound than anything he'd ever heard. A peace…

The mayor's call had shattered that peace, though. Too bad Hoge had charged his cell with the SUV battery. But, as sheriff, he could never go completely off the grid, just in case something happened that required his attention—although, fortunately, not a lot happened in Cold Creek.

Anymore…

"I'm here now," Hoge pointed out. "Anybody want to tell me why?"

Because it obviously had something to do with this woman. Then he remembered where he'd seen her—on TV, giving interviews—and he snapped his fingers in recognition. "You're the DNA scientist," he said. "The one who's been solving some seriously cold cases."

"And she's going to do the same here," Prentice said. His throat moved as if he was struggling hard to swallow for a second. Then he got out the rest of it, "...In Cold Creek."

Hoge dragged in a breath as if he'd been suckerpunched. He shook his head. "No."

Then he turned to leave. He had a few more days left of vacation and he intended to take them. He needed to go back to the woods, back to nature, to the peace he'd found there. Because he knew what the mayor had brought her here to dredge up...

And he had no intention of letting a stranger, even one who was as respected as Eve Collins, work *that* case.

"What does he mean?" Eve asked once the door had closed behind Sheriff Hogan Moore. "No?"

The mayor chuckled nervously. "I'm sure he was just joking."

Skeptical of Prentice's claim, Eve shook her head. "No. I don't think so."

The mayor sighed. "Well, you must have run into this before—a sheriff's stubborn stance against using science to solve cases."

She had. But usually those sheriffs had been closer to the mayor's age than her twenty-eight years. Not that she could be certain how old the sheriff was with that bushy beard concealing most of his face, and what it hadn't covered, his dark sunglasses had. There had not been a single strand of gray in his thick, long dark hair, though.

He'd also recognized her, so surely he had to respect what she did. He'd said himself that she'd solved some seriously cold cases.

Did he not think the cases in Cold Creek were seriously cold? The first murder had happened before Eve had even been born. Thirty years ago.

And then two years later there had been another and then four years later another.

Nothing since then. At least not in Cold Creek, Michigan. But Eve knew there had been at least one more murder, in another place, where another man had been blamed for this killer's crime.

She had to find the real killer. She had to find justice for those women who'd died and for the man who'd lost years of his life to prison because of him.

"I have had issues with some police departments and sheriff's offices in the past," she admitted.

"And you can't have even been doing this very long," the mayor said, "young as you are."

Unlike the sheriff, the mayor had not recognized her. She'd had to show him some of her references from other politicians and law enforcement branches before he'd recalled hearing about her. Even then, she hadn't believed he'd been truthful, just that he hadn't wanted to seem uninformed.

"I can handle the sheriff," she said.

Prentice shook his head, but not a single slicked-back blond hair moved. "You won't have to. I will make it clear to him that I brought you in to work these cases. He'll share all the evidence with you, whether he likes it or not."

"But…" she murmured as reluctance tugged at her. She didn't want to mislead the sheriff into thinking she worked for the mayor. Obviously the mayor had already misled himself into thinking that—despite that she was the one who'd come to him with the offer to work these cold cases.

Eve prided herself on always being open and honest—because unfortunately too many other people in her life hadn't been open and honest with her. This case was so important, though, that she would do whatever was necessary to solve it—even play along with the small-town politics she usually took great pains to avoid.

So she swallowed what she wanted to say and said instead, "Thank you, Mayor Prentice."

"Will any reporters be following your investigation?" he asked her, and he reached up to pat down his hair as if he expected one to be filming him right now.

She shook her head. "No." Because she had a feeling he intended to change that, she added, "I would hate for them to interfere in an ongoing investigation."

"Ongoing…" He snorted. "I doubt Hoge has looked at any of those cold cases since he took office two years ago. It really is good that you're here, Ms. Collins."

He hadn't acted that way, though, until she'd convinced him. But it was good for her. It was also good for those victims—all those victims of the killer—but it would not be good for the killer. This time, she would make certain that he was brought to justice for his crimes.

If he was still alive…

Unfortunately in too many previous cases, the DNA had led to dead ends—to killers already dead or in jail. And those cases she'd solved had never been prosecuted; the victims never got the justice they'd deserved.

The people wrongly accused had never been fully exonerated.

No. This killer had to be caught.

"Yes," she said. "It is good that I'm here."

She didn't even care if the mayor called in reporters like she suspected he would for publicity for his town as well as his next election. She just hoped he waited until she'd had time to complete her investigation. Just like Sheriff Moore didn't want her meddling in this case, she didn't want anyone meddling in it for her.

Chapter Two

Halfway to the cabin, Hoge had turned the SUV around and headed back to town. Even nature would not have cleared his mind and soul of all the tumult spiraling inside him now. Since that meeting...

Since that meeting, his cell kept vibrating where it sat on the console in his SUV. He let every one of the mayor's calls go directly to voice mail. He didn't even need to play the messages; he knew what Paul Prentice was saying.

Work with the DNA expert.

Solve those cases.

Nobody wanted those cases solved more than he did. But *he* wanted to be the one who solved them. And it wasn't just about pride or saving face or even carrying out his late father's dying wishes. These cases meant so much to him for another reason—a reason he was reluctant to admit even to himself.

But that reason was why Hoge *needed* to be the one who solved the murders, who found the killer...after all these years. Thirty years... Hoge had been alive when that first murder had been committed but just barely. He was thirty-one, almost thirty-two.

After stopping off at his house in town to shower and shave, he was feeling more like his age than as old and weary as he'd felt after that meeting. As refreshed as he was, he still didn't want to deal with the mayor.

Or with her...

So he sought out someone who could help him figure out how to deal with them, especially the mayor. After pulling the SUV to the curb outside a big Queen Anne–style house, the bed and breakfast in town, he threw open his door and headed toward the porch. But before he could climb the steps, the man he'd come to see was already on his way down them—a tall, broad man with a bald head that gleamed in the sunshine. Uncle Ted...

The consultant wasn't the only one who thought the cabin was too primitive. While Ted Prentice came up to fish during the day, he spent his nights at the B and B. He used to stay overnight, back when Rolland had been alive, but now he claimed he was getting too old.

"You're leaving?" Hoge asked.

"Like you, I got called back to work." Ted's brown eyes, warm with concern, studied his face. "But I can stay if you need me."

The pressure on Hoge's chest eased slightly. He wasn't as alone as he sometimes felt since his dad had passed away. He had Rolland Moore's friends; they cared about him. "Can you deal with your brother for me?"

Ted grinned. "You want me to give him a wedgie for you?"

Hoge chuckled, as his friend had obviously meant for him to do. "Would you, if I said yes?"

Ted laughed. "I would do anything for you, Hoge. You know that."

"I do," Hoge said, but there were some things he needed to do by himself, like solve those murders. "Go ahead, get back to work."

"I take it you have to do the same?" Ted asked.

Hoge nodded.

"Something happen?"

Eve Collins. She was what had happened. "Your brother hired a consultant."

"For what?" Ted asked.

"For those cold cases."

Ted reached out and gripped Hoge's shoulder. "Are you going to be okay?"

As close as Ted had been to Rolland Moore, he probably knew the truth…about Hoge. But they'd never talked about it, which Hoge appreciated.

He nodded and assured his honorary uncle, "I'm fine. Go ahead, get back to work." He had to do the same, and now after Ted had offered his support, Hoge felt a little less like he needed it. He felt a little more capable of dealing with the mayor and Ms. Collins. Just knowing that he wasn't as alone as he sometimes felt since his dad died made him stronger.

Ted studied his face for a long moment. Then he squeezed his shoulder again before pulling his hand away. "Let me know if you need anything…"

Patience. And faith…

That was all Hoge needed. After getting back into his SUV, he drove directly to the police department. When he pulled into the parking lot, he noticed the silver vehicle with a Pennsylvania license plate. It had been parked at city hall too.

It wasn't a stretch to conclude that the small hybrid was probably the consultant's. Cold Creek didn't get many out-of-state visitors since the town was so remote and so far north in the upper peninsula of Michigan.

So Eve Collins was here, probably waiting on that evidence. She wouldn't find it—at least not easily. His phone vibrated.

The mayor again.

Prentice wasn't going to give up. And neither would Hoge—no matter what he had to agree to solve the murders.

He clicked Accept. "Hello…"

"You're no longer ignoring my calls?"

"Obviously not," Hoge replied.

"That was childish of you," the mayor admonished him.

That was the trouble with having grown up in Cold Creek; not many of the townspeople took Hoge seriously as sheriff now, despite that the majority of them must've voted for him. It didn't matter that he'd graduated top of his class at the police academy or that he had a master's degree in criminology or six years of experience with the Detroit police department.

"I was showering," Hoge said. "And I'm technically still on vacation." Yet here he was, about to walk into the one-story fieldstone police department building.

"Hoge, I know this isn't ideal," the mayor surprisingly admitted. "Nobody wants an outsider getting into our business, but you've really left me no choice."

Hoge snorted. "How is that?" he asked.

"You've done nothing to solve these cases since you've been elected."

That was what Prentice thought, but the mayor didn't know nearly as much as he thought he did—because Hoge didn't want him to. There was so much Hoge didn't want anyone to realize. But now *she* was here...

"It hasn't seemed to be a problem for you until recently," he pointed out.

The mayor's sigh rattled the cell phone speaker. "I have been reluctant to open up all that pain of the past," he admitted—again, much to Hoge's surprise.

He'd suspected the mayor was more concerned about potentially poor publicity for the town, which could reflect badly on him, as well. Paul Prentice had big aspirations for state politics. But so far he'd lost every election in which he'd competed for a more prominent position and kept returning to Cold Creek.

"Then send her away," Hoge said. "She isn't going to solve our old cases." He'd struck out already at the state police lab, so Eve Collins was going to do nothing to help him solve these cases but slow him down even more re-running the same tests he'd already run.

"If we send her away, we look like we're hiding something," Paul said in protest.

Hoge shrugged. "Like what?"

"Like a killer," Paul replied.

Hoge sucked in a breath. Paul continued, his voice loud with authority. "That's what the consultant is going to think, what she'll probably tell reporters if you don't work with her. I'm sure the killer was just some transient passing through town."

"Three times?" Hoge asked quietly.

Three murders. Three young lives cut short too

soon and too cruelly—Loretta James, Amy Simpson
and Mary Torreson. All three women had gone missing
before they were found—strangled to death.

"We've had visitors who return to Cold Creek every
year," Paul said. "They rent the same cabins for fishing in the summer and hunting in the fall. Snowmobilers. Cross-country skiers in the winter. We are a tourist
town."

Hoge resisted the urge to snort at the ridiculous as-
sertion.

Tourist town?

Barely.

Sure, they had tourists but not nearly as many as the
mayor had insinuated, as many as Paul Prentice would
probably like to bring to town. He must have hired the
DNA expert to garner publicity. Hers wasn't going to
be the only out-of-state vehicle for long—if the mayor
had his way.

Now Hoge had to resist the urge to groan. He'd dealt
with enough reporters in Detroit. He didn't want to deal
with them here. He didn't want to deal with a consultant either.

But maybe the easiest way to get rid of the DNA scientist was to give her what she wanted. Once she realized her methods weren't going to solve these cases, she
would move on to the next ones, in some other town,
and some other sheriff would have to deal with her.

"I'm pulling in to the office now," Hoge told the
mayor, who was continuing to list potential murder suspects from bird-watching expeditions and color tours.

"My office?" Paul asked. "She's left—"

"My office," Hoge corrected him. "And I presume
she's here."

"She is very eager to get started processing the evidence," Paul said.

"It's already been processed."

"Years ago," Paul said. "And there have been so many recent advancements in science."

Hoge bit his bottom lip to hold back his comments. He didn't work for the mayor, so he hadn't kept him apprised of what he'd done. Of how much science he knew...

He sighed. "I'd better go. I don't want to keep her waiting. I have no idea if you're paying her by the hour or the case." He didn't expect the mayor to tell him, so he clicked off his phone.

Still he hesitated a long moment before opening the door of the SUV. He wasn't eager to see her again and it wasn't just because he owed her an apology over how abruptly he'd rejected her consulting on the case. He wasn't eager to open up the past with anyone, least of all a stranger who had no personal stake in what was very, very personal to Hoge.

"Don't take it personally," her father told Eve, his voice emanating from the cell phone she'd pressed tightly to her ear.

She'd kept her voice low as she talked to him. *Complained* to him, really, that the sheriff was refusing to work with her. But she probably hadn't needed to whisper; it wasn't as if anyone was eavesdropping on her conversation. She was the only person sitting in the small reception area of the stone-sided building that was the Cold Creek Police Department.

A woman, probably in her fifties from the faint lines around her dark eyes, sat behind a glass window in the wall that separated the small reception area from the back of the building. Like Eve, she was on a phone. She must have been the dispatcher. But she seemed to be making more calls than she was taking. The phone had only rung a couple of times during the hour Eve had been waiting for Sheriff Moore. The woman was supposed to have called the sheriff to let him know she was waiting, but Eve hadn't overheard her make that call. Instead she appeared to be on a personal call of her own, asking someone if they knew about the consultant the mayor had brought to town and adding that she didn't understand his bringing in an outsider.

Did no one want her here? She wasn't even really certain that the mayor did, just that Paul Prentice hadn't known how to turn down her offer without looking as if he was more interested in hiding the town's tragedies rather than actually solving those murders.

"But, Dad, nobody seems to realize that I'm not here to cause trouble. I'm only trying to help," she said.

His soft chuckle emanated from the phone now, drowning out another faint noise that barely caught Eve's attention. She ignored it as she listened to him. "I know who you're trying to help, my sweet Evie."

A smile tugged at her lips. "I wish you were here," she said. She needed him right now—to keep her focused and centered.

A door closed; it must have been the sound of it creaking open that she'd heard beneath her father's warm chuckle. She glanced up at the man who leaned against that closed door, staring down at her, and her heart did a little fluttery thing.

It was probably just because he'd caught her talking to her dad and surprised her. Not because the man was very attractive with a smoothly shaven square jaw and chiseled cheekbones and deep-set, heavily lashed eyes. He was very good-looking and very intense as he continued to stare at her.

"If you need me, I'll be there," her father promised— despite the other commitments she knew he had, the other people who needed him nearly as much as she did.

"I do need you," she said. "I miss you…" She had missed so much time with him—years that they could never make up. She bristled with anger over the lies that had kept them apart.

"I love you, sweetheart," her father said. "And God loves you. Everything will work out how it's meant to be."

"How can you…" How could he be so optimistic? So spiritual? Eve wanted to be, but she'd lost her faith—in justice and in humanity and sometimes even in God. But she couldn't say any of those things with the audience she had. The stranger's scrutiny unsettled her, making heat rush to her face. Why was he staring at her while obviously rudely eavesdropping on her conversation?

Lowering her voice even more, she said into the phone, "I'll talk to you later."

"The sheriff showed up," her father surmised.

The sheriff. That weird flutter moved through her chest again as she recognized that this man, with his thick dark hair, was the sheriff, cleanly showered and shaved. As usual, her father knew more than she did.

"Yes, the sheriff is here," she said.

She probably wouldn't have recognized him if her father's remark hadn't prompted her to take a closer look. He was the same height and build as the man she'd met briefly in the mayor's office, though he wore clean jeans and a crisp, tan uniform shirt now. And, as she'd suspected, he was young, probably not much older than she was.

"You'll win him over, sweetheart," her father said. "I love you."

"Love you too," she murmured as she clicked off the phone and jumped up from the hard, plastic chair where she'd been sitting for far too long.

"You didn't have to end your phone call with your boyfriend on my account," the sheriff remarked.

"Boyfriend?"

He arched a dark brow over one of those deep-set eyes. The irises were green—a very crisp, bright green like new leaves in the spring.

She shook her head. "That wasn't my boyfriend." She hadn't had one of those for a long while and with very good reason. "That was my father."

The sheriff's green eyes darkened and his broad shoulders bowed slightly. "Oh, then you definitely shouldn't have ended that call on my account."

She creased her forehead, then pushed up her glasses at his odd remark. "Why do you say that?"

He shrugged. "Just that…you never know how long you'll have your dad around."

She knew. Not nearly long enough.

Overwhelmed with emotion and the threat of tears rushing up the back of her throat, she only managed a nod. She fought back the tears, though, determined to be professional, more professional than the sheriff had been with her so far.

"And you shouldn't waste any of that time here, in Cold Creek," the sheriff continued.

She sighed. "So you're still refusing to work with me. Hasn't the mayor talked to you yet?"

He shook his head. "No."

"He said he was going—"

"That's not what I meant."

Eve had met a lot of lawmen since becoming a consultant five years ago. Some had even been as taciturn as the sheriff was. Usually she'd managed to hold on to her patience and grace, but she felt it slipping away from her now. Maybe it was because she felt as if she finally had a serious lead.

"What do you mean?" she asked.

Did he mean, no, he wasn't going to work with her? Or did this *no* mean he was no longer refusing to work with her?

Not that she actually wanted to work with him, and that wasn't just because he'd been so surly with her earlier. Eve preferred working alone, so she could focus only on the evidence and not the biases and prejudices of locals and law enforcement.

His green eyes narrowed, he tilted his head and stared at her. "What do you think I mean?" he asked.

"If you're refusing to work with me, it must mean that your ego is bigger than your need for justice for the victims and their families," she said.

His eyes widened now—probably with shock over her insult. And she had insulted him. She wanted to slap a hand over her mouth and shove her words back down, but it was too late. She'd offended the person she needed to work with to get access to the case files and evidence. She needed that access. Badly.

So she needed the sheriff's cooperation. But how could she appeal to his better nature? Did he have one?

"I'm sorry," she said, offering the apology in a rush. "I just feel really strongly that it doesn't matter how old a case is, that the killer could still be a danger to more innocent people. And that he has to be stopped for the safety of the public—so there are no more victims of his crimes and so that his previous victims are not forgotten." She sucked in a breath now and held it, waiting for his reply.

Would he work with her? Or would he send her away?

Chapter Three

"I hope you're not afraid of the dark," Hoge murmured as he led the way down the steep metal stairs to the basement.

"Of course not," the consultant replied.

That made one of them then.

Not that Hoge was exactly *afraid* of it anymore. Darkness just made him uneasy now—not terrified, like it had when he'd been a child. His father, having always been an honest man, hadn't dismissed his fears, hadn't told him that there was nothing to be afraid of in the darkness. They'd both known—even then—that there was plenty to fear. But his father had assuaged those fears with promises that he wouldn't let anyone or anything hurt Hoge.

And Rolland Moore had kept that promise.

His dad was gone now, though. He couldn't protect him anymore. Hoge was the protector now—of the town, his father's legacy and those long-dead victims.

"A lot of evidence lockers are in basements," Ms. Collins continued. "I've grown used to them."

He'd been in some of those evidence lockers as

well—in basements with poured concrete walls and high-tech ventilation systems. This basement was on the other end of the spectrum from those; it looked like it'd been made by dynamiting into a solid slab of stone over a hundred years ago, and it probably had been.

Jagged edges of rock jutted from the walls, and a dampness permeated the room and nearly everything in it but for those items stored in the old vault. The vault was so big that it never would have made it down the rickety metal staircase they descended now. The iron monstrosity must have been dropped into the space with a crane or a lot of man- or horsepower. The sheriff's office had once been a bank, and this was the vault for that bank.

Instead of holding the gold bars or valuables it had once held secure, it contained only evidence now. Hoge was one of very few people in possession of the code for the old lock. He turned the antique tumbler in the order of the numbers for that code, waiting until it clicked before pulling open the heavy steel door. Then he stepped back to allow the consultant to enter first.

She hesitated before stepping over the threshold. When the door opened, lights came on inside. She wasn't afraid of the dark, but maybe she was afraid of enclosed places.

That was another childhood phobia Hoge had had to overcome. And he had…

Mostly. He wasn't being entirely chivalrous to let her enter first, though. He could tolerate enclosed places as long as he wasn't alone. He was very aware that he wasn't alone—because he was very aware of Eve Collins, of the tresses of silky-looking blond hair that had slipped out of her bun to trail down her neck, of the sweet cinnamon scent emanating from her.

He could smell it because she hadn't moved away from him yet. She stood just outside the vault.

"Don't like small spaces?" he asked, wondering about *her* hesitation. He would have figured, eager as she was to see the evidence, that she would have rushed inside.

She glanced over her shoulder at him, a slight smile curving her lips, and asked, "You're not going to lock me inside, are you?"

He shuddered at the thought—not just of being locked inside but of being capable of such cruelty as to do that. That was the worst of all of his fears. "No."

"You've really changed your mind about my consulting on these cold cases then?" she asked with clear skepticism.

He had already decided, as he'd showered and shaved, to let her look at the evidence. But he hadn't had time to explain that to her upstairs, in the foyer, before she'd delivered her particularly impassioned speech about how victims deserved justice.

He wholeheartedly agreed with her, but he hadn't admitted anything to her. He'd only led her through the sheriff's office, past the holding cells, to the stairwell leading down to the basement.

He shrugged off his lingering doubts about her meddling in Cold Creek business. "I don't think you can help," he admitted. "But there's no harm in letting you look through the evidence."

In fact he counted on it changing her mind about working here. Once she saw that he'd already done what she usually did, she would realize he was right.

Behind her glasses, her eyes narrowed a bit as she studied his face. But she didn't argue with him; she just stepped inside the vault.

Old iron shelves lined the walls but many of them were empty.

"It shouldn't be too hard to find the evidence for those cases," she said as she peered around. "It doesn't look as if there are many boxes here."

"No. Cold Creek is a pretty quiet town," he said. "Just the usual drunk and disorderlies, petty thefts, property disputes…"

"And murder," she added when he trailed off.

"Not for a long time," he said, as he pulled out the first of the three boxes she would want. He didn't even need to look at the numbers on the box identifying the case it pertained to.

He knew.

A small, wooden table occupied the limited floor space in the middle of the vault. He set the box on it before reaching for the second and then the third.

Before lifting the lid from the first box, she pulled on plastic gloves she must have taken from the big leather bag she carried over her shoulder. The tote was bigger than a purse, bigger even than a briefcase. What else was in it?

Tools of her trade?

A DNA machine?

A microscope?

She used her glasses for now, peering through them at the contents of the box.

Dread gripped him, squeezing his stomach muscles, as she began to lift out the sealed evidence bags. The first contained a torn dress…stained with blood and tattered with age.

He closed his eyes for a moment, blocking out that image—that *memory*…

The sheriff's handsome face drained of all color, leaving him starkly pale.

"Are you okay?" Eve asked with concern. She'd suspected, when he'd asked about the dark and the small space, that those phobias were his. But how much did they affect him?

He opened his eyes, those vivid green eyes, and stared at her as if surprised to find her there, as if he'd forgotten all about her.

"Are you okay?" she asked again. "Do you need to sit down?" She glanced around but saw only the table and those shelves. No chairs.

He shook his head. "No. I'm fine. I think I probably forgot to eat today."

Probably. Eve's stomach would have never let her forget to eat; it rumbled now. She reached inside her bag and pulled out one of the granola bars she always carried with her and extended it to him.

He shook his head again. "No, I'm fine."

He was obviously lying to her. Being lied to by someone she trusted was her greatest phobia. But she didn't trust the sheriff. She really didn't trust anyone anymore, not after… She pushed her past back where it belonged—in the past—and focused on him again. "You don't look fine."

He drew in a deep breath before insisting, "I am."

Maybe he was lying out of some kind of misplaced male pride and not just to deceive her, like too many others had. Something about him made her want to give him the benefit of the doubt.

"You need to eat something," she said. "You probably have low blood sugar." She wouldn't know about that herself—she snacked too often. But snacking was easier than taking the time to cook and fix something for herself. She only took that time if her father was coming over.

"Are you going to look at the evidence or what?" the sheriff asked, his voice gruff with impatience.

"Here?" she asked.

"Where else would you look at it?" But his question was rhetorical, because he continued, "You can't take it out of here. It has to remain in the custody of the sheriff's office until we forward it to the district attorney to file charges."

"I've signed out evidence in other cases," she informed him.

But clearly, he wasn't willing to let her do that in this case. He seemed to be very protective of what had happened so many years before he'd been elected sheriff. Maybe she wasn't the only one with a personal connection to the murders.

She continued, "It's never been an issue with previous district attorneys because I was able to verify that I had maintained the chain of evidence when I testified."

Unfortunately she hadn't had to testify that often. Few district attorneys had brought charges in the cases she'd solved—either because the perpetrators had been dead or were already in prison for other convictions.

"And," she persisted, "I will need to bring the evidence into a lab to extract and test whatever DNA I find."

"You don't have a microscope in that suitcase you

carry around with you?" he asked, his tone almost teasing now.

She shook her head. She had a magnifying glass in her bag, though. "Even if I did, I would still need the DNA sequencing machine, and that's a little too big to carry around with me." Although the equipment got smaller all the time, with every technological advancement. Fortunately the processing time got faster too.

"You don't need it," he told her. "Everything has already been tested. Recently, too. I had the state lab rerun the DNA through all the databases."

Those test results were what had drawn her here—to Cold Creek, Michigan. She just hadn't realized, until now, who had requested to have those tests run. After the sheriff's reaction in the mayor's office, Eve had assumed it must have been the state police cold-case unit or the district attorney for Cold Creek. She'd been wrong about that, and the mayor had been wrong about Sheriff Moore's disinterest in the cases. He'd known almost instinctively what boxes had held the evidence for each of them.

"I will need to test it again," she said, "to confirm any matches I might make."

Creases furrowed his brow. "Matches to what?" he asked. "Do you have any suspects?"

Frustration gnawing at her that she didn't have any, she shook her head. "No. I meant matches to other cases."

His green eyes widened with apparent surprise. "He's killed more than these three women?"

She nodded.

At least one. There might have been more—if he'd gotten better at leaving no DNA behind, and maybe he'd gotten so good that his victims weren't even found anymore. So many women went missing all the time…

"Who? Where? How many?" he fired the questions at her as if she'd suddenly become a suspect.

"I know of one for sure," she said. "From eighteen years ago. Samantha Otten was only twenty years old, working as a secretary at an insurance office in Philadelphia during the day while attending college at night."

A frown crossed his handsome face. "So young, like the victims here in Cold Creek."

She nodded. "The DNA the killer left at Samantha's crime scene matches the DNA left at the crime scenes in Cold Creek."

"I had the DNA run against possible perpetrators, not other cases," the sheriff expounded. "He's not in the system. He's never been caught."

"Not yet," she said. "But he will be…" She was going to make certain that he was finally brought to justice for all the crimes he'd committed. For the murders but also for framing an innocent man, for stealing years of that man's life as well as his reputation.

"How?" the sheriff asked, his tone challenging, and color had returned to his face.

"He's left DNA behind," she said.

"But what are you going to match it to when he's not in the system?" he asked. "Without any suspects, you can't get a warrant from a judge for a DNA sample."

"There are ancestry databases," she reminded him of how some killers had recently been caught. "Although I have run his profile through a few of them, and I haven't got any matches yet."

"I don't think a killer would be putting his DNA out

there in ancestry databases, not now when it's been so publicized that's how some have gotten caught."

"It's not the killers who've submitted their DNA but their family members," she said. "And we can use that to build a family tree of sorts for this killer—to find out where he fits into it." Or she could have if she'd located any of his family members in the ancestry databases. But none of them had submitted their DNA either. Was that because they were protecting him?

Or were they just older or not interested? She intended to keep checking to see if someone finally sent in a sample that related to his profile.

"Won't you need a court order?" the sheriff asked. "Those companies have lost so many customers that they're filing for privacy protections for their clients now."

She'd been denied access to the ancestry sites a couple of times now, so she uttered a weary sigh. "What are you saying then?" she asked. "That these cases are unsolvable? That the killer will never be caught?" She couldn't—she *wouldn't*—accept that.

"No. I'm saying that you won't catch him." His mouth curved into a slight grin. "*I* will."

An answering smile tugged at her lips. He definitely had more than his share of macho male pride. "How?" she asked as she upended the contents of that first box onto the table. "With this? There isn't much here to go on…"

"For science, there isn't," he agreed. "But for real police work, there is."

"Real police work?" she asked. "What do you consider real police work?"

"Interviewing witnesses, tracking down suspects, questioning them…"

"Beating confessions out of them with rubber hoses?" she asked. "It's been thirty years since that first murder. Are the witnesses still alive?"

The color drained from his face again. Maybe arguing with her had lowered his blood sugar even more.

"Sheriff?" she called out to him in concern. She didn't want to work with him, but she didn't want anything to happen to him either.

He glanced at her with that same look, like he'd forgotten she was there for a moment. "What?"

"Are the witnesses still alive?" she repeated. "Were any suspects questioned?" And was the killer still alive? Or had he died with everyone believing that he was an innocent man and not the monster he truly was?

Sheriff Moore pointed toward the boxes. "Everything you need to know is there." He turned toward the door then, walking away from her.

She didn't believe him, and it wasn't just because she didn't trust easily anymore. There was something he wasn't telling her—something significant. What was it?

"Sheriff?" she called out as he stepped through the doorway to the vault.

He didn't turn back to her, just paused outside the door. "I'm not shutting you inside," he assured her. "I'm just going to get something to eat."

"I offered you a granola bar," she reminded him.

"Thank you," he said. "But I need something more substantial than oats right now."

Did he really need to eat? Or was it that these old cases affected him for some reason?

He turned back to her. "When you're done looking

through that stuff, you can just close the door to the vault and it'll lock automatically."

"You're really not going to let me take anything out of here?" she asked. "I thought you'd changed your mind about cooperating with me."

"This is me cooperating," he insisted even as he walked away.

She'd wanted access to the evidence, and he'd given her that—even if he wouldn't let her bring it to her own laboratory. But for some reason she wanted more than the evidence.

Like the sheriff had said, it was going to take more than the lab tests they'd both already completed to solve this case. Eve didn't know anything *but* science; she didn't know how to find suspects without it. But he did...

Chapter Four

Hoge hadn't lied to the consultant when he'd told her he hadn't eaten that day. Despite that, he couldn't summon any interest in the plate of food the waitress had slid across the scratched but polished table in the corner booth he'd taken at the Cold Creek Café. His stomach churned at the sight of grease oozing from the burger, saturating the bun and the thick French fries piled next to it.

Usually he liked burgers the greasier the better. But not right now.

Not with that consultant rummaging through the old case files. What was her interest in the murders? Was she just seeking justice, like she'd claimed? Or was she hoping to further her career with publicity?

Not that there had been much of that over the years. His father, the former sheriff, was the only one who'd really stayed determined to solve the cases. The rest of Cold Creek had seemed to want to forget that the murders had ever happened, that that horror had ever touched their town.

As well as not having much media coverage, there wasn't much evidence either. So Hoge wasn't surprised to glance up and see Ms. Collins walking through the café door and heading straight toward his booth.

His booth...

The café owner reserved it for him. Not with a sign or anything, but with an intimidating glare if anyone else tried sitting at it. It had always been like that, always been reserved for the sheriff of Cold Creek.

The booth had been his father's first and for many decades. It was where Rolland Moore had hung out with his friends and the locals, drinking coffee and swapping stories. Sometimes, when Hoge sat here, he could almost hear the echo of his father's deep voice, the rumble of his chuckle...

"Sheriff!" the consultant called out, her voice sharp with impatience as if she was tired of trying to get his attention.

She had it. She'd had it from the moment he'd stepped into the mayor's office. Eve Collins was incredibly attractive. And from her reputation, she was even more incredibly smart and determined.

"Ms. Collins," he acknowledged her, then asked, "Did you decide you want more than oats too?"

She furrowed her brow and stared at him in confusion. "What?"

He gestured at his burger. "You want something more substantial than your granola bar?" He'd gladly hand over his plate if she wanted it. He sure didn't, especially now—especially when he knew she'd sought him out for a reason. To talk about the evidence or the pitiful lack of it?

Resigned to the fact that he had to deal with her—at least until he convinced her to give up—he pointed toward the other side of the booth. "Have a seat."

She hesitated for a moment before sliding across the vinyl, her bag clutched against her side. Had she smuggled out some of the evidence in that bag?

Given the amount they had, most of it would probably fit inside it. He shoved his plate across the table. "Have my burger."

She studied it for a moment, as if tempted, before shaking her head and pushing it back toward him. "You haven't touched it," she said. "You need to eat. You're still so pale."

He reached up to run a hand along his recently shaven jaw. "I just look that way because the sun couldn't get through my beard."

She narrowed her eyes as if skeptical of his claim before slowly nodding in agreement. "It was pretty bushy."

"Bushy," he said. "Nothing pretty about it." Not like her…

She was very pretty with that pale blond hair and her bright blue eyes. The black-rimmed glasses only somehow highlighted her natural beauty. Too bad she'd come to Cold Creek to investigate those murders.

Not that he would have asked her out even if she hadn't. He'd determined long ago that relationships weren't worth the risk. Staying single like Uncle Ted was better than having his heart broken like his father had. Or worse…breaking someone else's heart. He was afraid, with his focus on his job, that he wouldn't be able to give a significant other the time and attention she deserved .

No. The only relationship he could have with Eve Collins was a professional one, and if he thought she could actually help him solve the cold cases, he would have welcomed her involvement. But he knew that with her came reporters and other unwanted publicity. At least unwanted by him…

The mayor would undoubtedly revel in all the attention to the town and to him—because somehow Paul Prentice would make it all about himself. Hoge groaned.

And she reached across the table to touch the back of his hand. "You really aren't feeling well," she surmised.

He glanced down at her hand on his, marveling at how his skin tingled from the contact. Maybe she'd felt it too because she snatched her hand back across the table and tucked it beneath the surface.

"I'm fine," he assured her. "Just tired…"

"But you were just on vacation," she reminded him. "Did all that nature at your primitive cabin wear you out?"

"It's not my vacation that wore me out," he said with a pointed glance at her.

She sighed in frustration. "I don't understand why you don't want my help."

"I don't need it," he replied with the blunt honesty that had gotten him into trouble in the past—with politicians like Paul Prentice and with superiors at his prior police department in Detroit. "I've already had the state police run the same tests on the evidence that you can run."

"But there are more tests that will need to be run," she said.

He peered across the table, at the bag that took up more of her side of the booth than her slender body did. "You didn't take anything from the vault, did you?"

Her eyes widened behind her lenses. "What?"

Was her innocence real or feigned?

"Do I need to get a search warrant for your bag?" he wondered aloud.

She lifted it onto the table next to his plate. "You don't need a search warrant. Be my guest. All you'll find inside are some more snacks and—" her face flushed with color "—other things…"

He had no interest in her personal things or in her personally. Not really…

"I didn't take any of the evidence," she said. "Although what there is of it would fit easily inside my bag."

Despite having had the thought himself, he flinched. There should have been more evidence. "I warned you," he said. "There's nothing you can do here, nothing that I haven't already had done. Sorry that you wasted your time coming to Cold Creek, Ms. Collins."

She flinched now but shook her head. "It's not a waste of time. It's just going to take longer. I'll have to find suspects whose DNA I can run against the evidence."

"You'll have to find them?" he asked. "You're a scientist, Ms. Collins, not a detective."

Her face flushed again with the spots of color on her cheeks turning from pink to red. "Uh…"

He tilted his head and waited.

"You may not need me," she said. "But I need you."

His pulse quickened—even though he knew she wasn't implying anything beyond professionally. But he was still surprised that she'd admitted to needing his help. Maybe he wasn't the only bluntly honest person at his booth.

Eve had had no interest in the sheriff's burger, but she nearly reached for his glass of ice water. She was tempted to fish out some of the cubes to press against her hot face. "I—I meant that I need you…" She nearly bit her tongue as she said it again.

His deep chuckle interrupted her. "I know what you mean," he said.

But she wondered if he did…

Had she given him the wrong impression? She was always so careful to behave professionally and not just when she was working. She'd worked hard to build walls to protect herself from getting her heart broken again like it had been broken when a few of the people she'd trusted most had lied to her. Her mother, her fiancé, her best friend…

She knew she should be able to forgive. It was the Christian thing to do, the thing her father wanted most for her. But she couldn't bring herself to do that yet, if ever. And she would never, ever forget.

"I need to make myself clear," she said, so that there was no confusion…or anything else…between them. "I just want to do my job. I want to close these cold cases."

"Why?" he asked, and his green eyes narrowed as he stared at her.

She nearly shivered under his scrutiny. It was almost as if he knew she had a personal stake in these cases, in this killer. "Because it's my job," she replied, as if that should have been obvious to him. And it should have been, but somehow he'd astutely surmised she had another reason.

"Why?" he asked again.

She groaned. "You sound like a three-year-old I used to babysit…" And she nearly groaned again over probably offending him. Usually she could be more diplomatic, but this case—this *killer*—mattered too much.

He shrugged, as if letting the unintended insult drop

off his broad shoulders. Hogan Moore was a big man, muscular, but he hadn't intimidated her until now, until his inquisition. He leaned over the table and remarked, "And you sound like a suspect reluctant to answer my questions because you might give away your guilt."

"I'm not guilty of anything," she assured him. Except maybe not being entirely honest, which was so against her nature and her beliefs that more heat rushed into her face with a wave of the guilt she'd just denied.

"Then why won't you answer my questions?" he mused.

"Is this how you interrogate suspects?" she asked. Because if it was, she'd definitely been right when she'd told him that she needed him.

He chuckled again. "Are you a suspect?" he asked.

"For some reason you're treating me like one," she pointed out.

"I do wonder why you're so determined to work this investigation," he said. "There can't be much opportunity for national news coverage of some cold cases in a podunk town in the upper peninsula of Michigan."

"I don't look for publicity," she told him. The media attention had always unnerved her.

"What do you look for?" he asked.

"Killers," she replied.

"You said that last murder happened in Pennsylvania, and I noticed the plate on your car is also Pennsylvania. Any connection?" he asked.

"No," she replied. She wasn't entirely lying, since she wasn't connected to the victim. And she wasn't connected to the real killer, the one whose DNA had finally been extracted from the evidence to clear the man who'd spent a decade in prison...

"But I did start working that case first," she admitted. She didn't add, though, how long she'd been working that case or why. Clearly he was looking for a reason to refuse her help and her personal involvement might be reason enough. "That case led me here," she said, "to Cold Creek."

He continued to study her, as if he suspected she had ulterior motives. Sheriff Hogan Moore was smart.

Eve was glad that she'd pestered the dispatcher until the older woman had relented and told her where the sheriff was. But when she'd learned he was probably in *his* booth at the local diner, she'd worried that he was more like the mayor had implied than he'd appeared in the vault.

That he wasn't really interested in justice. That he spent the majority of his time gossiping at the local café and fishing. That he wasn't very good at his job.

But she suspected the mayor was wrong about Sheriff Moore. From the way he was interrogating her, she had a feeling that he was very good at his job. She needed him to find the suspects and to interrogate them because those were things that she couldn't do.

But how could she convince him that he needed her? Tell him the truth? The whole truth?

She was worried if she did that, though, that he would consider her too involved in the case to be objective. Or worst yet, that her personal connection might provide a defense for the killer's lawyer.

Revenge...

Chapter Five

He was going to regret this. He knew it. But Hoge uttered a weary sigh and relented. "Okay…"

Her blue eyes brightened and she leaned across the table toward him. "Okay?"

He nodded. "You have me, Ms. Collins," he replied, deliberately teasing her. But when he said it, something shifted inside him, something almost as unsettling as working those cold cases with someone else. But when she'd said her focus was finding killers…

He believed her. He believed she cared about that more than publicity. He suspected she had reasons why—reasons she wasn't willing to admit. But so did he.

So he wasn't going to judge. He was going to leave that to someone else once the killer was found. And he wanted that killer found even more than the consultant did. Whatever her motivation was, it couldn't be as powerful or as personal as his. Closing those cold cases was more than keeping a promise to his father— so much more…

She clapped her hands together. "Where do we start?

Did you have any suspects that weren't mentioned in the files?"

No suspects had been mentioned in the files. Over the past three decades, no one of interest had ever really turned up. He shook his head. "What about you? That other case you mentioned, was there a suspect?"

The color drained from her face, leaving her suddenly and starkly pale.

"What?" he asked. "What is it?"

And why hadn't he been more interested when she'd mentioned it? Obviously there was a lead there.

But she shook her head. "There wasn't any viable suspect, nobody whose DNA matched what was found at the crime scene."

"Nobody?" he asked, disappointment adding to the weight already on his shoulders.

She shook her head again. "No. There wasn't much other evidence besides that DNA."

"So we're not the only ones who hadn't found any viable suspects," he said. But that didn't make him feel any better, just more hopeless.

"The key—the clues—to finding him has to be here in Cold Creek," she insisted.

"Why?" he asked.

"Because these were the first murders and there were more than one."

"So there is only one other murder where his DNA was left," he said.

She nodded. "Six years after the last one here."

"And then nothing?" he asked.

"I wouldn't say nothing," she said. "I think he just got better at it. He either didn't leave DNA behind or he didn't even leave bodies behind. Too many women disappear and are never found."

He sucked in a breath and nodded. "I know. Or he could have just stopped."

She shook her head. "The only way to be certain that he isn't killing anymore is to find out who he is."

"So you think these first three murders are significant because…" He knew but he didn't want to say it; he'd rather accept the mayor's theory about the transient.

Before he could pose it, though, the consultant was already answering him. "I think he started here because he grew up here or has lived here a very long time."

"You think the killer is a Cold Creek resident," he murmured as his stomach churned. He pushed the plate with the burger even farther away. The pool of grease had coagulated into a sticky white substance.

"Hey, Sheriff, something wrong with the burger?"

He glanced up at the man who'd asked the question. He hadn't heard Lenny approach, which was odd since the man was so large. Lenny had tattoos etched on his bald head, his neck and his brawny arms.

Ms. Collins's slim body stiffened and she glanced surreptitiously at the café's cook. Was she nervous of him because of his appearance or because she suspected that every man in Cold Creek might be a killer?

Hoge offered the man a smile. "It's fine, Lenny," he assured him, and he wanted to assure her, too, that the cook wasn't a killer.

Hoge was probably the only man she couldn't suspect because he wasn't old enough to have committed those murders. Lenny probably was, although he would have had to start in his teens. From the research Hoge had done, he knew that most serial killers started in their teens even if just with animals. That bothered Hoge nearly as much as killing humans, though. He inwardly cringed over the times he'd done it himself.

"I thought you'd be dying for some bloody red meat after eating just fish for the past couple of weeks," Lenny remarked. Despite being a hunter, Hoge didn't believe in hurting any of God's creatures—unless it was done as humanely as possible and for a source of food. And even then, it bothered him.

Lenny was a hunter too. But was it just for food or because he enjoyed the kill?

Now Eve had him looking at people the way she was. Hoge grimaced. "I was, but I'm suddenly not feeling very hungry. I think I must have caught something…" Like the mayor's hired consultant messing in his cold cases, but he'd agreed to her interference now. No wonder Prentice preferred to think an outsider had committed the murders. That made more sense to Hoge than someone he knew being a killer. His father would have figured that out years ago and caught him.

So the killer had to have been a seasonal visitor.

How would they track him down then? Hoge would need help, so maybe agreeing to work with Ms. Collins wasn't the mistake he worried it was.

"I just made a fresh batch of chicken noodle soup," Lenny said. "That'll settle your stomach." He turned toward the consultant. "And what about you, Miss? Would you like anything? I see the waitress hasn't stopped by your booth yet."

Hoge glanced around to find every table filled. While he'd been focused on the consultant, the café had gotten busy—too busy to spare Lenny from the kitchen.

Was he just curious about the stranger? Or was it

more than that? Had he heard about her arrival to town already?

Hoge suspected his dispatcher, Doreen, had made certain most of the town had been apprised of who Eve Collins was and what her intentions were in Cold Creek.

To solve those old cases...

Why?

Hoge suspected there was more to her reason than she'd claimed. But he didn't care really. All he cared about was finally solving the murders and closing those cases.

So that he could keep his promise to his father and to himself and...

Ms. Collins shook her head and managed a smile for Lenny as she murmured, "No, thank you."

Lenny turned back toward him. "I gotta get back in the kitchen. I'll send the waitress out with that bowl of soup for you," he said as he grabbed up Hoge's untouched plate. He rushed off before Hoge could stop him.

"You really get some service here," Ms. Collins remarked. "At *your* table."

He sighed. "Doreen..."

"The dispatcher?"

He nodded.

"It wasn't easy for me to get her to crack and actually speak to me," Ms. Collins assured him.

"That's a first," he said.

"Maybe it's because I'm an outsider," she said.

He nodded and reminded her, "That's why you *need* me."

She shook her head but she was smiling. "You know how I meant that."

"I do." But he liked teasing her. He wasn't sure why, but he felt like the little boy she'd accused him of being, the one who'd tugged on Melinda Powers's long blond ponytail because he'd thought she was cute.

She was married now and usually pregnant, while Hoge remained single and was usually alone. Although someone usually joined him when he sat at this booth, they only shared a meal with him. No one shared his life.

That was the way it had to be, and not just so he could give all his time and attention to his job but also because of those cold cases.

For some reason he wasn't all that eager to get started on them now, though, despite Eve Collins nudging him. Maybe it was because he had no idea where to start, where to find those suspects whose DNA she needed to match to the pathetic amount of evidence left at those murder scenes. The three here and the one that had brought her to Cold Creek.

"You're staying here to eat?" she asked with a glance around the diner. People looked away as she caught them staring at her.

Hoge smiled. That was probably why the place had suddenly gotten so busy—because of her. They all wanted to see the consultant who'd come to town. Then he looked again at the faces that were all familiar to him. Bob Dempski sat with Alice, the mayor's secretary. He felt a flash of guilt for accusing Doreen of gossiping. Maybe one of those two had spread the news about Ms. Collins. A chill raced down his spine to think that anyone in the café could actually be a killer...

He couldn't allow himself to think so badly of people he knew. It wasn't what his father and his faith had taught him. Shame hung heavily on his shoulders.

"You told me I should," he reminded her. But he wasn't sure he'd be able to enjoy the bowl of soup either, not with all the turmoil rushing over him.

She nodded. "You should, but we also need to get started."

"In the morning," he said as he glanced toward the windows. The light was fading outside. Then he asked, "Where are you staying?"

She shrugged. "Local hotel, I guess."

He chuckled and shook his head. "I might rethink that if I were you."

"Why?"

"Let's just say you've probably seen cleaner crime scenes than those rooms."

"I've seen some very clean crime scenes," she remarked. "Killers are getting smart."

"This killer?" he asked.

She nodded. "I think so."

"You really think he's still killing?" That would explain her urgency, an urgency that coursed through him too.

"I don't think someone like this stops until he gets stopped," she said.

That was probably the reason for her determination in finding him—to save lives. As sheriff, that was Hoge's primary reason as well, but he had other ones.

"I think we'll both be able to focus better in the morning," he said, knowing that they wouldn't easily identify suspects, or he would have already.

"So where should I stay?" she asked him. "Any recommendations?"

"I know of a few rental cabins."

She grimaced. "I like indoor plumbing."

He grinned. "I don't rent out my cabin." He liked to protect his space. His cases…

So why had he agreed to work with her?

Because justice was the most important thing, and it didn't matter how he finally got it for those victims. Sure, he would have preferred to handle it on his own, but he'd had two years to work those cases and hadn't made any progress. He sighed.

He'd been working those cases even longer than that and had proved unsuccessful in solving them. Was there a part of him that didn't want to know the truth?

"I want to stay in town," she said.

"Not into nature?" he asked, and disappointment tugged at him that something so important to him might not be important to her. Not that it mattered. They were just working together, so that was the only thing they needed to have in common. Work.

"I'm into convenience," she said.

Then he pointed out the window toward the large Queen Anne home across the street. "The bed-and-breakfast has clean rooms and good muffins. They offer a cheaper rate if you stay more than three nights."

And he suspected she would be in Cold Creek longer than that…unless she was even better at her job than he'd heard. He hoped she was. Not that he wanted her gone so soon.

He just wanted these cases finally closed.

The sheriff was right. The rooms were clean, and even though it was well past breakfast, Eve had received a plate of muffins with packets of soft butter when she'd checked into the local B and B. That plate sat on the bedside table, just a few crumbs and a smear of butter left on the blue-and-white china.

After sliding her empty suitcase beneath the clothes she'd hung in the closet, she closed the door and leaned back against it. Crisp white linens covered the bed, along with a duvet cover with small yellow flowers embroidered on it, which matched the curtains hanging over the window. The room was clean and except for the soft tick of the clock sitting next to the empty plate, it was quiet. Elsewhere in the big house, a TV rumbled and a fan whirred, so she wasn't alone.

But she felt alone—*alone*—and somehow vulnerable. Since building walls around herself, she didn't often feel that way. Maybe it was how everyone had been staring at her in the café. Or how she was just so certain that *he* had to be here…the *killer*…

Had he been in the café? Was he one of the people who'd been staring at her? Could it have been the cook? Had he come out of the kitchen with genuine concern for the sheriff or with curiosity over her? And was that place always so busy on a weeknight or had they all been checking her out, wondering if she would find the killer…

Maybe one of them had wondered if she would find out that the killer was *him*. Whoever he was…

A chill rushed over her, and she shivered. Was she that unnerved by the thought of being so close to a killer? She'd been closer before—when a court order had given her the authority to swab for DNA. But then police officers had been present as well, and ready to protect her if necessary. Could she trust anyone here to protect her?

The sheriff had only begrudgingly agreed to work with her, but she had no doubt that he really didn't welcome what he saw as her intrusion in his investigation. Such as it was.

He'd done more than the mayor had thought he'd done, but not much more. Not enough to find a killer. He probably didn't want to believe there was a killer in the town where he lived, the town he was supposed to protect. But she was pretty sure there was, or at least there had been.

Was he still here?

Was he still alive?

Still free?

Unlike the ten years another man had not been free, because of him, because of his crime. She probably should have shared that with the sheriff when he'd asked about other suspects for the murder in Pennsylvania, but she'd answered honestly. Despite going to jail for the crime, the man hadn't been guilty, which DNA evidence had proven ten years too late. So he hadn't been a viable suspect no matter what police, a judge and a jury had once thought.

That chill persisted, making her shiver again. She could have reached into the closet for the cardigan dangling from one of the hangers. But instead she reached for her cell, and she called the one person she could trust: her father.

"I'm glad you called back, sweetheart," he said. "I've been worrying about you."

She would have told him that she was fine, but she wouldn't lie to her father, just as *he* had never lied to her. He was one of the few who'd always been honest with her unlike her mother and fiancé and former best friend…

And maybe even Hogan Moore. She suspected he was still keeping something from her. "The sheriff agreed to work with me."

"That's good," he said. "I think."

She was equally uncertain. "He showed me the evidence," she said. "Such as it was…"

"You've gone through it all already?" he asked.

"There wasn't much, and he'd already had the state lab run tests on the DNA he had," she said.

"So you're coming home to Pittsburgh," he said.

"No, I'm staying," she said.

"But why?"

"The killer is here, Dad," she said. "I just know he is."

"No," he corrected her. "You *want* him to be. You want to find him so bad that it's becoming an obsession for you, Evie. It's not healthy."

"I'm fine," she said, flinching with the twinge of guilt that struck her over the lie.

"You're a young woman with no social life," he said. "All you do is work. That's not healthy. You need more."

"I have you," she reminded him. Now. But she'd been denied him for too long.

"You need more," he told her.

She glanced down at her left hand; it was naked now but had once had a ring on it. Not anymore, not after she'd discovered that her fiancé and her best friend had been more than friends. While he'd promised he could wait until marriage for her—because of her faith—he hadn't been willing to wait until marriage for himself. She'd thought they'd had the same values, the same beliefs. She'd thought the same of her best friend, until she'd caught them together. While she still held the same values and beliefs, she'd lost a bit of her faith…in other people and maybe even a little in God.

Why did so many terrible things happen to good people? It wasn't fair. How could He allow such unfairness?

Despite knowing why she didn't have most relationships any longer, her father continued. "You need friends. A fella…"

For some reason the sheriff's face flashed into her mind, cleanly shaven with those deep green eyes. She shook the image from her head. "I don't need anyone." But that was another lie. She needed her father, and she needed God, no matter how much she struggled with her faith from time to time. She'd also told the sheriff she needed him. But she just needed his help finding suspects whose DNA she could test.

"We all need someone, Evie," her father said. "We're not meant to be alone."

"Then what about you?" she asked. "Are you seeing someone besides the inmates you counsel?"

Bruce Collins was a minister at the local maximum-security prison. Somehow, despite everything he'd endured, he'd kept his faith and continued to share it. But she had no idea how he was able to keep going back there…to a place where he never should have been. Eve wished she was as strong as her father was. As good…

He chuckled. "Okay. You've caught me in my hypocrisy. I'm sorry, darling. I just want you to be happy."

"I will be," she said, "when this killer is caught."

His sigh rattled her cell phone speaker. "What if that doesn't happen?" he asked. "What if you can't find him? Will you never be happy then?"

She couldn't consider the possibility. "I will find

him. I will." She had to. "And I need a good night's rest to do that," she said. "So I'd better let you go."

Like she'd had to so long ago.

But she had him back now. "I love you, Dad," she told him.

"I love you, my darling," he replied. "And because I do, I will continue to worry about you and pray for you."

He wasn't the only one. She was worried, too, even more so after their conversation. Maybe she should have prayed with him like the inmates did, but she wouldn't have prayed for herself. She would have prayed, as she had so many times before, to find a killer. After disconnecting the call, she got out her toiletry bag and nightgown and headed to the bathroom. Fortunately the B and B had all en suite rooms, so she didn't need to share. She could spread her stuff out across the small countertop because she suspected she might be here awhile.

Once she was ready for bed, she turned on a light in the bathroom but closed the door. The light would remind her where it was if she woke up in the middle of the night, disoriented, as she sometimes did because she traveled so often. But the light reminded her of the sheriff, of his wondering if she was afraid of the dark.

Why had he asked that? And why did she keep thinking about him? Shaking thoughts of him from her mind, she turned down the blankets and crawled into bed, but as she flipped off the lamp, she noticed light seeping in under the door to the hall. It didn't illuminate just the hardwood floor but a white envelope, as well.

It couldn't be a bill. She'd told the proprietress that she would be staying for more than a night, probably more than a few nights. So what was it?

She flipped the lamp back on and walked toward the

door, bent down and retrieved the envelope. Then she carried it back to the bed. The envelope wasn't sealed—its flap lay open exposing a sheet of plain lined paper. She pulled out the paper and unfolded it. A single sentence had been scrawled across it—*If you want to live, you need to leave Cold Creek.*

That chill she'd felt earlier raced over her skin again, raising goose bumps along her flesh as her heart pounded. But along with the fear coursing through her was excitement.

She was right. The killer was here and he was still alive. Still free…

For now. But now she was even more determined to find him—to provide justice for all the killer's victims and to protect herself from becoming the next victim.

Chapter Six

Even though the hybrid with the Pennsylvania plate wasn't parked in the lot, Hoge wasn't surprised to walk into the sheriff's department and find the consultant waiting for him again.

Juggling his travel coffee mug and sunglasses, he opened the door to the interior offices and leaned against it, holding it open to allow her to pass him. He would have to tell Doreen that it was all right for her to let Ms. Collins back. Maybe he'd even have to give the consultant an office space of her own somewhere in the building—far from his.

She jumped up from her seat and hustled past him, the bag swinging from her shoulder nearly knocking his coffee and his sunglasses from his grasp. After last night, he really needed his coffee.

He certainly hadn't had any sleep.

"You are really eager to solve these cases," he remarked.

"Aren't you?" she asked, glancing over her shoulder at him.

He gestured for her to head down the hall and murmured, "More than you know..." Especially after last night...after the nightmares had come back. Not that they'd ever really stopped since they'd started all those years ago—when he'd been just a kid. But he hadn't had them as frequently over the years as he'd had when he was little, when all those feelings had rushed over him in the dark.

The panic—the fear—clawed at him now, making it hard for him to draw a breath. But finally he managed to suck in some air.

"What did you say?" she asked. "I missed that."

He shook his head. "You didn't miss anything..."

He suspected that she seldom did; that was why she was so well-known. Frustration gripped him now, like the panic and fear had last night. Unlike her, he must have missed something in that evidence, in what he personally knew, or he would have solved these cases long before the mayor had had to hire help.

Hoge was still a little surprised that Paul Prentice had hired her. Since Prentice had taken office, four years before Hoge had taken his as sheriff, the mayor had seemed more determined for everyone to forget that the old murders had ever occurred than to open them up all over again. That was why Hoge hadn't told him that he'd had the state rerun labs on all the evidence. He hadn't wanted to deal with what he'd suspected would be the mayor's vehement disapproval.

Ms. Collins had stopped outside his office door. Hoge juggled his coffee cup and cell phone in the same hand as he pushed open the door for her.

Her face flushed. "I—I thought you would have locked it," she said, "or I would have opened it for you."

Before he could move his coffee cup back to his free

hand, his cell phone began to vibrate against it, slosh-
ing coffee out of the sipping hole. The hot black liq-
uid splashed over his fingers, making him wince from
the burn.

Ms. Collins grabbed the cup from his hand and
walked inside to place it on his desk. "Are you okay?"

He nodded as he glanced down at the cell screen,
on which droplets of coffee had also spattered. Maybe
his thinking about the mayor had somehow manifested
Paul Prentice's call.

Hoge must not have answered it fast enough, though,
because the vibrating stopped. He released a short sigh.

But then her bag began to buzz, and she grimaced.
Before she even pulled her cell from her purse, Hoge
knew who was calling her.

"The mayor," she murmured.

Clearly she was thinking about purposely ignoring it.
Her brow furrowed above the black rims of her glasses.
Then she sighed and clicked the accept button. "Eve
Collins, how may I help you?" she asked, as if she didn't
already know who was calling her.

More furrows creased her brow as she listened. Hoge
couldn't hear what the mayor was saying, only her side
of the conversation. But from that he could just about
guess.

"No, Mr. Prentice, the sheriff wasn't ignoring your
call," she defended him to the mayor. "He didn't have
a chance to answer it before you hung up."

Hoge smiled at her subtle rebuke.

"Yes, he has agreed to work with me," she continued.
"We were hoping to get started right—"

The mayor must have interrupted her like Hoge had
been tempted to do. He wasn't sure he wanted to get

started right away—not when he knew where this investigation was going to lead them.

Lead *him*…

Back to his past. Back into the nightmares that had interrupted his sleep last night. But maybe the only way to stop those nightmares from recurring was to finally solve those cases and catch the murderer.

Eve was really going to have to make it clear to the mayor that she did not work for him. She wasn't even sure he was going to pay her since she'd essentially volunteered for this assignment. But, not wanting to have that conversation in front of the sheriff, Eve hadn't been able to argue her way out of this meeting the mayor had insisted on having with the two of them.

Just as he'd called the sheriff back from his vacation, he'd summoned them both to his office. Why? She'd told him—or she'd tried telling him—that they were just getting started on working the cases. He couldn't be expecting results already.

"Are you missing that three-year-old now?" the sheriff asked.

Eve peered across the console at his chiseled profile. Since she'd left her vehicle in the B and B parking lot, the sheriff had offered her a ride to city hall. "What?"

"That one you used to babysit?" he asked. "The one who asked all the questions."

A smile tugged at her lips. "You're comparing the mayor to the three-year-old now?"

He nodded. "Aren't you?"

"He is as impatient as one," she admitted. "I hope he doesn't think we have any results yet." Although she did, in a way, in that note she'd tucked into an evidence bag. It was in her purse. She'd intended to show it to the sheriff, but she hadn't had a chance.

And she wasn't entirely certain that she should…

It was meant to scare her off, and she wasn't going anywhere. Not until the killer was caught. That was why she'd left her car in the parking lot behind the bed-and-breakfast and walked to the sheriff's office—to show *him* that she wasn't afraid of him. Of course she'd had a can of pepper spray clutched tightly in her hand… just in case…

She was more scared of what might happen if she shared that note with the sheriff, though. He might use it as an excuse to get rid of her, stating that her involvement was too dangerous. Could he have slid that note under her door last night, trying to get her off the case?

She narrowed her eyes and studied his handsome face even more. His brow was furrowed, his mouth pulled into a slight frown—the same one he'd been wearing when she'd told him that the mayor insisted they both come to his office right away.

When she'd told him about the meeting, he'd muttered something beneath his breath that could have been curses…except that she'd recognized the words as a prayer…for patience.

It was one she often heartfeltly recited herself. From the tension clearly gripping him, she suspected the prayer hadn't worked yet for him.

A smile tugged at her lips now. Sheriff Hogan Moore was an interesting man. Not that she was interested in him. Her only interest in Cold Creek was in finding a killer. And she didn't want to waste another minute before getting started on the investigation.

"Why do you think he wants to see us?" she asked.

The sheriff arched a dark brow. "He didn't say?"

She shook her head, but his focus was on the windshield as he steered into the parking lot of city hall. So she replied, "He didn't. He just insisted it was important."

The sheriff pulled into a parking spot and shut off the SUV. "Guess we'll know soon enough what he wants." But something about the sheriff's tone suggested he already knew or at least had a pretty good idea. And since his frown deepened, drawing tight lines next to his mouth, he wasn't particularly thrilled.

Neither was she, but she opened her door and stepped out into the parking lot. The sheriff took a moment longer before joining her on the asphalt. Perhaps he'd muttered another prayer for patience.

Eve silently recited the words of it, as well. She'd already been patient so long, though, and to be so close and not able to actually work the case yet…her patience could not be tested more than it was being tested right now, which also tested her faith. Why was justice so hard to obtain?

The sheriff drew in a deep breath, bracing himself as he pulled open the door to city hall. Eve drew in a breath of her own, one that smelled like the sheriff—like outdoors and musk and masculinity—before stepping through the door he held open for her.

The gray-haired security guard greeted the sheriff with a big grin, but the grin slipped away when he looked at her. He'd been friendlier when she'd arrived yesterday, but then he hadn't known why she was here. Thanks to Doreen, or maybe the mayor himself, he must have learned her reason.

But why would that make him unfriendly? Unless…

Did he have something to hide? As she peered at him, he looked away, as if unwilling to meet her gaze.

"We have a meeting with the mayor, Bob," the sheriff explained their presence.

The man didn't bother searching them, just nodded and allowed them to enter. The sheriff headed for the stairs but stopped. "Would you prefer the elevator?"

She shook her head. The stairs were probably faster given that the mayor's office was only two floors up. And she was in a hurry. Grateful she'd worn flats, she darted up the two flights into the open reception area of the third floor.

The mayor's secretary was already looking up, as if she'd been waiting for them. Or maybe she'd heard the sound of the sheriff's heavy footsteps on the marble treads. She greeted them both with a smile, albeit a bit sheepish one. "He's waiting for you," she said with a slight sigh.

"Is he alone today?" the sheriff asked.

Again, sheepishly, the woman shook her head, and now her gaze dropped from theirs. She wasn't going to tell them who was with him. But now Eve had a sinking feeling in her stomach, which was already heavy with the lemon poppy-seed muffins she'd scarfed down for breakfast.

She glanced up at the sheriff's face. Along with his frown, he clenched his jaw so tightly she could almost hear his teeth grinding. Just wanting this meeting over already, she headed toward the office door. She opened it before the sheriff—who'd been so chivalrous with doors—could even reach for it. The mayor was not alone. An older man and a younger woman sat in the chairs in front of his desk. They turned at her and the sheriff's entrance.

"There you are!" the mayor exclaimed. "We've been waiting."

All of ten minutes at the most. City hall was not far from the sheriff's department. Prentice was far more like that little boy she used to babysit than the sheriff was. She turned to make sure Hogan Moore had actually stepped into the room with her. He hesitated in the doorway instead.

"Marshall, Brooke..." he greeted the mayor's visitors, but his tone wasn't any warmer than it had been when he'd met her yesterday.

"You know the sheriff," the mayor said, dismissively. "Ms. Collins is who I wanted you to meet. She's a renowned scientist responsible for solving many cold cases, just as she will be solving the Cold Creek murders."

Eve offered a tentative smile as she tilted her head, waiting for the introductions. The young, dark haired woman popped up from her chair to shake Eve's hand.

"I'm Brooke Oliver, and I'm thrilled to meet you," she said. "When the mayor called yesterday, I looked up your career. So impressive."

The older man remained sitting, his shoulders stiff and his mouth pulled into an even bigger frown than the sheriff's. He didn't look any happier to be here than Eve or Sheriff Moore were. She wanted to be working on those cases, delving more deeply into the evidence, looking for suspects.

Not wanting to be rude, Eve shook the woman's hand and smiled at her. But then she turned to the mayor.

"I don't understand what this meeting is about…" Or who these people were.

"This is a press conference," the mayor explained. "These are representatives of our local paper and online television station. They'll be following your investigation, and once they file their stories, I'm sure the national news will come to Cold Creek to cover it, as well."

Eve suppressed a groan. He was obviously counting on the national news coming. Struggling for that patience for which she'd prayed, she carefully reminded him, "This is not what we discussed yesterday."

"It doesn't matter what you decided," the sheriff interjected. "No reporters are allowed to cover an ongoing police investigation—"

The mayor snorted. "There's nothing ongoing about your investigation into these murders, Hoge, and we all know it."

"That's not true," Eve said, jumping to his defense.

The sheriff remained firm. "As I said, I'm not keeping reporters apprised of an ongoing investigation. They'll be informed once the cases are solved."

"You had no hope of solving them until now," the mayor said. "Until I hired Ms. Collins—"

The sheriff wasn't listening, though; he turned and walked out, letting the door swing shut behind him. Eve reached for the door handle to follow him out.

"Ms. Collins," the mayor said. "We're in the middle of a press conference."

She shook her head. "No, you are. I agree with the sheriff. We'll report to you once we have something to report." She turned the knob and hurried out after him.

Had he left her? The trip from the sheriff's office

to city hall hadn't been long, but she'd still rather not walk it. He was waiting for her in the foyer, talking to the guard, their voices pitched low.

"That was fast," he remarked. "Get all your publicity photos taken?"

She shook her head. "I didn't know he'd called reporters."

"I thought you discussed it yesterday," he said, tossing her words back at her.

"I told him not to call them," she said. "That they would only hinder the investigation."

He smirked. "Yeah, right…" He waved at the guard as he headed toward the doors to the parking lot.

Eve rushed out with him. "I'm not lying," she insisted. "I don't want the reporters following our investigation either."

"The press is how you've built your reputation," he said.

Her pride stinging, she corrected him, "Solving cases is how I've built my reputation."

"But you wouldn't even get to work those cases if you didn't have a reputation," he said. "If your successes hadn't been so widely publicized. It's clear now that you're in this for the glory."

She sucked in a breath, feeling like he'd slapped her. "As I told you before, I am in this for the justice."

"Justice for whom?" he asked.

She was tempted to tell him—to tell him everything. But then he would refuse to work with her, probably using some excuse about her personal connection, which he might claim was a quest for revenge, messing up a potential prosecution. She was certain that he was looking for any excuse to get out of working with her. So she probably shouldn't tell him about the note either.

His phone rang then, and he grimaced. "If Prentice is…" But when he pulled out the cell, he shook his head. "It's not him." He clicked on the phone, but it wasn't on Speaker.

She had no idea who had called him, and his expression and the few words he spoke gave away nothing.

When he clicked off, he murmured, "I need to drop you back at the B and B."

"What? Why?" Had he found the excuse he was looking for?

"I have to go out on a call," he said. "I don't know how long it might take."

"Sheriff—"

He shook his head. "I have a job to do," he said. "And current cases take precedence over the old ones."

She wondered, though, if there really was a new case. He'd said yesterday that nothing much ever happened in Cold Creek besides drunk and disorderlies and petty thefts. It was a little too early for anyone to have gotten drunk yet. But in case it was the latter…

"I'll walk back to the B and B," she offered. "You go out on your call."

"Are you sure?" he asked. He pulled open the door to his SUV, and the police radio crackled with disjointed voices. Something really was going on.

She nodded. "Very sure. Current cases take precedence. Let me know when you get back." She had a feeling she shouldn't hold her breath waiting for him to do that, though. Despite agreeing to work with her, he was still clearly wary of her.

He wasn't the only one. Eve was wary of him too. He

was the one who'd sent her to the B and B, so it would have been easy for him to slip that note beneath her door. Easy for him to warn her away from cases where he'd not welcomed her involvement. Why?

She doubted that he meant her any actual harm, like the note had threatened. If he'd left it, he had probably just wanted to scare her away from Cold Creek.

What was he worried about? Her taking the *glory* for solving the cases? Or of the cases finally being solved and the killer caught? He was too young to have been the killer, but he wasn't too young to know the killer. Was it someone close to him? Someone he was trying to protect?

Chapter Seven

"That was some long police call."

Startled at the sound of Ms. Collins's soft voice, Hoge bumped his knee against his desk. He glanced up to find her standing in his office doorway, her arms crossed. The morning sun streaking through the blinds shimmered in her blond hair. Maybe he shouldn't have told Doreen it was okay to let her come straight back.

Noting that she had circles nearly as dark as her frames rimming her eyes, he mused, "Hope you didn't wait up for me all of last night."

She glared at him. "I knew not to hold my breath waiting for you to call."

"I really was busy late into the evening," he said.

"I hope it wasn't anything too serious," she said, and she sounded sincere.

His face heated slightly. He'd been busy, but it hadn't been particularly serious. Kids skipping school and hanging out on the railroad tracks. Fortunately the tracks were abandoned, so nobody had been at risk of getting killed—just hurt—especially when he'd discovered they'd sneaked out some of their fathers' alcohol too.

He sighed. "It was small-town sheriffing at its finest," he admitted. "I had to round up some rebellious teenagers and lecture them."

She arched a blond brow above the frames of her glasses. "Did you speak to them from experience?"

He laughed at the thought of doing what they'd done. "No way. I could *not* get into trouble like that."

"Why not?" she asked. "Always on the fast track to being sheriff one day?"

"Always the sheriff's son," he said.

Her blue eyes widened in surprise, but then she nodded. "It all makes sense now."

"What makes sense now?" he asked.

"Why you were so reluctant for my help on these cases," she said. "You think your father should have solved them."

Clearly she thought that. So had Rolland Moore. Leaving those cases unsolved had been his biggest deathbed regret, and so Hoge had promised that he would close them. *He* would even if he had to have the help of a consultant.

Hoge bristled with defensiveness—of his father and of himself. "He tried," he defended his father first. Rolland Moore had been a good lawman and an even better man. "He was busy."

She arched a blond brow again. "Really. You said nothing much happens in Cold Creek…"

"He didn't have the budget to have the number of deputies to help him that I do," Hoge said. "And he was raising me on his own."

She clasped a hand over her mouth, but it was already too late to hold back what she'd said. "I'm sorry. I didn't know your mother is dead."

"I didn't say she is," he pointed out. "I just said he raised me alone." His father's marriage falling apart was another reason Hoge knew not to risk the institution himself. If Rolland Moore hadn't been able to make it work…

Her brow furrowed beneath her wispy blond bangs. "And you obviously don't want to talk about it."

"I don't," he confirmed. Not with her or with anyone else. "And I didn't think you did either. I thought you were eager to get working on these cases."

She narrowed her eyes in a slight glare then. "*I* am. I would like to solve them."

"So would I," he said. And not just so he could keep the promise to his father but also because he *needed* to know himself. Who was the killer?

She clapped her hands together then. "So where do we get started?" she asked. "Do we go back to the crime scenes? Do we talk to whatever witnesses might have been around, if not during the crimes, at least around the times of the murders? And we should really talk to the victims' families too."

They would have to do all that; Hoge knew it, but he wasn't quite ready for it. "We should review all the evidence together first."

Not that he was thrilled to do that either, but now he wanted to see her reaction to every piece of it, see if she saw anything he'd missed.

"Why?" she asked. "You've already had tests run on the evidence you have. We have to find viable suspects. Do you remember who was in town during the murders?"

"I was a baby," he pointed out.

Her face flushed. "Yes, of course. But you must know someone who would know, someone who's lived here all their lives too."

"Just because there were three murders here doesn't mean that the killer is a Cold Creek resident," he said, and now he was defending his town.

"It sure makes every Cold Creek resident a suspect, though." She shivered. "At least the men."

"Not me." He pointed out, "I'm too young."

"And too reluctant to want to consider all the viable suspects. Do *you* have an idea who it is?" Then she narrowed her eyes, intently studying his face, and asked, "Are you trying to protect someone?"

He sucked in a breath, shocked and offended that she would suggest such a thing. "I'm a lawman," he reminded her. "I would never protect a killer."

He shook his head. "So, of course not. I just think there are viable suspects other than town residents. It could be someone who has visited here a lot. We have fishermen and hunters and snowmobilers who come every season." He nearly flinched at hearing how like the mayor he sounded, but he really didn't want the killer to be a Cold Creek resident, to be someone he knew.

"Is it any of those seasons right now?" she asked with a little quaver in her voice. Of excitement? Or fear?

He studied her face now, wondering what she was getting at…what she might know and how. Did she know something he didn't? "What do you mean?"

"Well, there's no snow, so it's not snowmobiling season. I don't think hunting season starts for a bit either. As for fishing, I guess that happens whenever, so maybe the killer could be a fisherman," she said and there was almost a triumphant tone to her voice when she added, "because something has happened now."

Shock struck him again, hard, like a slap across the face that had his neck snapping back. "What has happened now?" he asked. "It sounds like you're implying that the killer has done something, like he's here now. But how can you know…"

Unless another body had turned up. Had another woman been murdered?

Eve had been afraid to show the sheriff the note. She still didn't trust him entirely. But the frustration gripping her overruled her mistrust. "You are so determined to believe the killer isn't in town, but you're wrong."

"How can you know that for certain?" he asked, his green eyes wide with alarm. "Has someone been killed? Attacked?"

She shook her head. "No, but I've been threatened." She pulled the plastic evidence bag from her purse and dropped it onto his desk.

If he'd slid the note beneath her door, he didn't appear to recognize it now. His brow creased with lines of confusion and concern as he stared through the transparent bag at the threat written across the paper. "When— how—did you receive this?" he asked.

She released a shaky breath that she hadn't even realized she'd been holding since showing him the note. "It was slipped under my door shortly after I took a room at the B and B."

"Two nights ago?" he asked.

She nodded.

"Why didn't you call me then?" he asked.

"I don't have your number," she said.

"It's 9-1-1," he said. "And ask for me. You know that. Why wouldn't you call and report this threat the minute you received it?"

She shrugged. "I wasn't sure how you'd react," she admitted honestly. And in the spirit of that honesty, she added, "Or even if you were the one who'd written it." She still wasn't entirely certain that he wasn't.

His eyes widened with shock. "What? You think I would threaten you? Why?"

"I don't think you'd really hurt me. But I think you might want to get me to leave town. You've made it very clear that you'd rather I didn't get involved in these cases," she pointed out.

"Because I don't need your help," he said. "Not because I have anything personal against you."

She snorted. "Yeah, right. You think I only do my job for the *glory.* And if you didn't need my help, these cases would have already been solved."

Color flushed his face. She wasn't certain if he was angry or embarrassed that they'd remained open all these years.

"You must know how difficult some cases can be to solve," he said, his voice gruff.

"Especially when you refuse to acknowledge that the killer must be someone you know," she said.

He shook his head. "You don't know that."

She pointed toward the note. "The killer is here—in Cold Creek."

"You don't know for certain that the killer wrote this note," the sheriff said. "A minute ago you said you thought I did it, and I'm too young to have committed those murders."

"No. I don't know for certain that the killer wrote it," she admitted. "But whoever wrote it clearly wants me to leave town." She wasn't the interrogator she suspected he was from when he'd questioned her intentions in the diner, but she studied his face when she asked him point-blank, "Did you write it?"

His head snapped back, as if she'd slapped him. "Absolutely not," he succinctly replied with such outrage that she nearly believed him.

Nearly—because she'd believed people before that she shouldn't have. After the pain of her mother's betrayal and her broken engagement, she'd learned to be more cautious. If she trusted the wrong person now, doing the work she'd chosen, she might get more than a broken heart.

"I don't recognize the handwriting either, but I will find out who wrote it," he vowed as he picked up the evidence bag and started around his desk.

Before he could walk out the door with it, Eve stepped into his path and blocked him. "How?" she asked. "There are no fingerprints on it. I already checked." And since the flap of the envelope hadn't been licked, she'd found no DNA either.

"I'll find out using old-fashioned police work," he replied and he moved forward, bringing his body so close to hers that she could almost feel the tension in him.

She was tense, too, with fear and frustration and something else…an awareness of the sheriff that she didn't want to have. She quickly stepped away from him.

"If this note is from the killer, we'll find him through it," he said.

Eve had hoped so too until she'd concluded that no

fingerprints or DNA had been left on it. "But there's nothing to go on."

Just as he'd begun to leave no evidence behind of his crimes. Had the killer gotten that good? So good that it would be impossible to catch him?

The sheriff was undeterred, though, as he strode out of his office, the evidence bag clutched in one tight fist. Maybe he did have a suspect in mind after all. Or at least he knew where to look…probably at the B and B where the note had been left. Where Eve had tried, unsuccessfully, to sleep the past two nights. Instead she'd lain awake, wondering if the killer had left that note for her and waiting for him to threaten her again. Either with another note.

Or…

With an attempt on her life like he'd taken the lives of those other women. But Eve hadn't been about to make it easy for him. She'd pushed a dresser in front of the door, and she'd clutched her can of pepper spray like the sheriff now clutched the note.

She'd protected herself. She'd learned, the hard way, to do that now. But there was something about the sheriff rushing off to her defense that warmed her heart, that made it beat nearly as fast as the threat had.

And that was another kind of threat entirely…

Chapter Eight

Horror gripped Hoge. Horror that Eve Collins had been threatened, and horror that she had suspected him of writing the note. Had he been that unwelcoming? That difficult to her? He must have been, since she'd been afraid to come to him for help and had suffered alone.

Except that she didn't seem as scared as she was angry...but for those dark circles beneath her eyes. Now he knew why they were there, why she hadn't been sleeping. She'd been waiting for the killer to make good on his threat.

Hoge was going to make certain that didn't happen, that she stayed safe. And to keep her safe, he had to keep her close while he went back to the B and B to investigate. Once again she'd walked to the police department that morning, so he'd insisted she ride with him back to the old Queen Anne.

She'd agreed, so hopefully she'd gotten over her suspicion that he might have written that note. Her thinking that he might have threatened her, that he might have threatened anyone, turned his stomach. And she didn't even know…

He glanced across the SUV console at her profile and asked, "Why are you taking such chances?"

"Chances?" she repeated.

"Walking to the department," he said. "For two days now…" He shuddered as he remembered yesterday he had let her walk from city hall to the B and B. But if he'd known…

He would have let one of his deputies handle those wayward teens, and he would have made sure she stayed safe. But she hadn't trusted him enough to confide in him.

He pulled the SUV to the curb outside the B and B and glanced over at her again.

Color had suffused her face, painting bright pink spots on her cheeks. "I—I didn't want him to think that he actually scared me," she said.

"Him or me?" he wondered aloud. "I really didn't write that note."

She studied his face for a long moment before nodding as if she accepted his word. But doubts still dimmed the brightness of her blue eyes. She didn't trust him.

He couldn't blame her, though. He didn't trust easily either, or he wouldn't have suspected her reasons for being here.

What was her agenda?

Just justice, like she claimed? Had she really not wanted anything to do with the reporters the mayor had gathered yesterday for his sad, little press conference?

"I should have left you back at the police department," he said. "You'd be safer there."

She shook her head. "I don't care about my safety," she said. "I care about catching a murderer."

"You can't do that if you're dead," he pointed out.

"I don't believe he really intends to kill me," she said. "He just wants to scare me away."

"If he is the one who wrote the note, he's killed before," Hoge said. "So there is every reason to believe that he will kill again."

"That's why we need to find him," she said. "And stop him."

He nodded in agreement. That was most important—making sure that nobody else was hurt. Especially not Eve Collins.

There was something about her—suspicions and all—that drew Hoge. It was more than her beauty, more than her intelligence, even. Maybe it was her determination, her grit.

Clearly she knew exactly what she wanted and who she was. If only he could say the same...

She opened the passenger door and stepped out onto the sidewalk. He jumped out of the driver's door and hurried around to her side of the SUV, making certain to step between her and the old house, from where the killer might be watching them even now.

"I told you that there was no evidence left," she said. "We would be better off looking into those murders than this threat."

"Those murders happened years ago," he said. "This threat just happened. We're more likely to find witnesses here—at the B and B—than we are to crimes that occurred so long ago."

Her lips parted on a slight gasp. "Of course, I wasn't thinking..."

"No, you weren't," he agreed. "You should have come to me right away. That witness we need might have already checked out." Or maybe the killer had if he'd been staying here too.

Not that the B and B probably did all that much business, although the color tours would be starting soon. The leaves were just beginning to change from green to yellows and oranges and reds, and mums, in all those same hues, had been planted alongside the brick path that led to the front porch of the B and B.

Hoge stayed close to Ms. Collins as they walked that path, up the steps and across the porch to the tall arched front door. He pushed it open and stepped into the foyer. Except for several antique pieces of furniture, the area and the parlor adjacent to it were empty. He walked up to the dark oak desk and tapped the little brass bell that sat atop it. Seconds after its tinkle rang out, a gray-haired woman appeared in the doorway behind the desk, wiping her hands on a dish towel.

"Hello, Sheriff." Mrs. Watson greeted him with a smile. "I've been meaning to thank you for referring Ms. Collins to us." She smiled at the consultant, too, with none of the curiosity the rest of the town had shown her.

Of course Mrs. Watson and her husband, Mike, hadn't been in town that long. They'd purchased the B and B just a few years ago when they'd retired from their jobs in the hotel industry in Detroit. Hoge had known them in Detroit and recommended the town to them. He hadn't told them then about those long-ago murders, but someone had probably filled them in on the gossip by now. So, like everyone else, she had to know why the mayor had brought a consultant to Cold Creek.

"Hi, Pam," he greeted the B and B owner. "And call me Hoge."

Her smile widened. "I don't feel right doing that anymore," she said. "Not when everyone else calls you Sheriff."

Despite being elected two years ago, he wasn't used to it yet either. Every time someone addressed him as such, he had the knee-jerk reaction of looking around for his father, even though Rolland Moore had passed away more than two years ago.

"I am here in my sheriff capacity," he admitted.

Her dark eyes widened in surprise. "Really? I thought you might just be looking for some of those orange cranberry muffins you love so much."

She glanced from him to Ms. Collins and from their faces, she must have discerned that he was serious. "What is it?" she asked with concern. "What's happened?"

As Ms. Collins had placed the note on his desk, he placed it on Pam's. She pulled up the glasses from the chain around her neck and peered through the lenses. "Oh, my…" she murmured. "Where did this come from?"

"Here," he informed her. "Ms. Collins found it under her door two nights ago."

"When you first checked in?" Pam asked with concern. "Why didn't you say anything to me?"

A smile tugged at his lips as Ms. Collins's face flushed again over the same question he'd asked. He wasn't amused over what had happened, though, just over the irony of Pam asking the same thing he had.

Could Eve have suspected her innkeeper of slipping the note under her door? Or perhaps Pam's husband? It seemed no one was safe from Eve Collins's suspicions. What had made her so cynical? Her job or something more personal?

"I intended to speak to the sheriff about it first," Ms. Collins replied. "But we were interrupted yesterday."

A twinge of regret struck him. That had been his fault then. He could have delegated that police call to a deputy, but after the mayor's *press* conference, he hadn't been willing to trust her either.

"I'm sorry that this happened," Pam replied. "I can't imagine who would have written such a thing." She couldn't—despite all her years of living in the big city—but Eve had easily imagined everyone capable of having put that note under her door.

Even him…

Or maybe most especially him. His twinge of regret turned to shame over not having been more welcoming to her, about working with her.

"Can I take a look at the guest registry?" he asked. "I need to see who had access to her room."

"Nobody has keys but the guests, me and Mike," Pam replied. But she pulled open a desk drawer and lifted out her laptop. "Old habit has me wanting you to get a warrant, Sheriff—Hoge. But this is my establishment. My rules." She turned toward Ms. Collins. "My guests. I want you to be safe." She opened up the laptop and turned it toward Hoge with a spreadsheet listing the date, the room number and the guest name.

His eyes widened with shock as he recognized several names on the spreadsheet. "Lenny's staying here?"

Eve gasped. "The cook from the café?"

Pam smiled. "Yes, he says the landlord is doing repairs on his apartment, but I think he's trying to figure out the recipes for my muffins."

"And Bob?" he asked, adding for Eve's sake, "The guard at city hall."

Pam's smile slid away. "Bob and his wife are having some problems. I think it's why he went back to work after retiring from the police department."

Bob had stepped into the sheriff's shoes after cancer had taken Rolland Moore from Cold Creek. But he hadn't run against Hoge in the election; he'd retired instead only to start working again, a few weeks later, at city hall.

Pam sighed. "Apparently Margaret wanted more space from him and suggested he check in here for a while."

"And Marshall..."

"The reporter?" Eve asked.

Hoge nodded.

"He checked in the same day Ms. Collins did," Pam said, smiling again. "Grumbling about the mayor calling him away from his cabin to work on something for him. Sound familiar?"

Bob had probably filled in Pam about how unhappy Hoge had been to have his vacation cut short by the mayor's order to city hall.

"And his brother checked out that same day," Pam replied.

"The reporter's brother?" Eve asked, her brow creasing with confusion.

Pam shook her head and pointed toward the register. "Ted Prentice. The mayor's brother. Even though he was fishing with Hoge, he stays here more than at the cabin when he comes home to Cold Creek. Once you were called to town, he checked out."

"He had to go back to work," Hoge murmured.

"Why didn't he stay with the mayor?" Eve asked.

"They're not close," Hoge admitted. Ted had had much more in common with Hoge's father than his own brother.

"How well do you know him?" Eve asked. "How well do you know any of them?"

Every muscle in Hoge's body tensed with defensiveness and dread. "I've known them all my whole life," he said. "None of them wrote that note." But he wished Pam had had her guests sign a registry book, so he could have compared handwriting. It didn't matter, though; he refused to believe that one of the men he'd known, who had been friends with his father, could be a killer.

"I'll talk to them," he promised. "Maybe one of them saw who slid the note under your door."

"It had to be one of them," Eve persisted. "Who else would have had access to the house?" She looked at the proprietress then.

Pam's face flushed. "I've been living in Cold Creek long enough that I've gotten out of the habit of locking doors," she admitted. "Especially with Lenny living here. He comes in late, and if he's misplaced his key, I don't want him waking everyone else up."

"So anyone could have gotten into the house," Hoge pointed out. But his tension didn't ease any; his stomach muscles were knotted from it, his shoulders ached with it—from the burden he'd been carrying for so long.

He wanted—he *needed*—to solve these cold cases. It was the only thing that would ease that burden and end his nightmares. Or make them worse…

No matter what, though, he couldn't risk Eve's safety to close this investigation. He thanked Pam for her help and, with his hand on her elbow, guided Eve back through the foyer to the front porch. "You need to leave here," he told her.

"And go where?" she asked. "The motel. You told me the rooms look worse than crime scenes."

But he was afraid that if she stayed here, her room would become a crime scene—that she would become the newest victim of the killer they both sought.

"You need to leave—not just the B and B," he said. "You need to leave Cold Creek."

Eve laughed, her voice echoing off the blue bead-board ceiling of the B and B's front porch.

"You think this is funny?" the sheriff asked, his mouth pulled into a frown again. Even frowning, he was handsome.

Eve shrugged off the errant thought and his comment. "I think it's funny that you think you can order me out of town like some old-time sheriff. You can't make me leave here."

"I can refuse to work with you," he pointed out.

"That's why I didn't want to tell you about the note," she admitted. "I know you're looking for an excuse to stop my investigation."

He released a ragged sigh. "You thought I threatened you to get you to leave."

She nodded. "I know you don't want me here. You don't want to solve these cases."

"*I* do," he said.

She laughed again as she finally realized what his

problem was. "And you accused me of wanting the glory. You want it. You want all the credit."

He shook his head. "That's not it. I just…"

"What?" she asked when he trailed off. "Why don't you want to work with me, especially now?"

"Especially when you're in danger?" he asked.

"Especially when we're so close," she said, excitement coursing through her. "I can get DNA from the other guests. I can see if it matches the killer's."

"I doubt one of the other guests is the killer," he said.

"Then I'm perfectly safe here," she pointed out.

He groaned. "Eve…"

It was the first time he'd used her first name, and a little thrill shot through her. No. Chill. It scared her that he was getting familiar with her, familiar to her. Except for her father, the only other people close to her had hurt her. Badly.

"You heard Pam say that she doesn't lock the doors," he said. "You know you're not safe here."

"I don't care," she said. "Not when we're this close to finally having a viable lead."

"Your safety is most important right now," he said.

"Sheriff—" She refused to use his first name.

"Listen to the sheriff," a deep voice interjected, and she turned to find a man standing at the bottom of the steps leading up to the porch. He was tall with his hair cut short in a still more pepper than salt buzz cut. "He's right. Your safety is the most important thing, Evie."

She nearly flung herself down the stairs in her haste to reach him and throw her arms around him. "Dad!"

"Evie, you're shaking," he murmured as he patted her back.

She hadn't realized how unnerved that note had

made her…until she'd seen him. But seeing him and his siding with the sheriff wasn't going to make her leave; it just reinforced all the reasons she had to stay.

That she had to find the killer…

Chapter Nine

Would she come back to the office? Would Eve Collins say goodbye to Hoge? Or would she just pack up and leave with her father?

After she'd introduced the tall, lean stranger to him, Hoge had left them alone together. He figured she would listen to her father…like he'd always listened to his. Her joy over seeing Bruce Collins had moved something in Hoge, something in his heart.

Maybe it had just been envy. Or maybe empathy…

Maybe they had more in common than he'd realized. They were into family. Fathers at least.

He had never known his mother. Rolland had made sure that Hoge had never felt like he'd missed anything, though. He'd been both father and mother, protector and friend. Hoge missed him so much.

And even though he'd only known Ms. Collins for a couple of days, Hoge suspected he would miss her, as well. At least he would miss her fresh perspective and even her unfounded suspicions. She made him look at everyone and everything differently, and while that wasn't necessarily a good thing, maybe that was what it would take for him to solve these murders. Because he hadn't managed to do that yet despite all the years he'd known about and worked the cases.

He was in the evidence vault now, poring over the contents of the boxes he'd dumped onto that table in the middle of the space. The table was small, but it was big enough to hold the pathetic scraps of clothes and hair samples taken from the crime scenes.

And the photos…

He hadn't looked at them yet. He always needed to brace himself before he did. But when he drew in a deep breath and reached for them, a creaking noise startled him. His breath whooshed out, and he moved toward the open door of the vault.

Despite the dim light in the basement, he could easily distinguish the person descending the metal stairs to join him. Her pale hair shimmered in the flickering fluorescent bulbs. He really needed to replace those with more energy-efficient lighting.

But that was the least of his concerns at the moment. When she joined him just outside the vault, he asked, "Are you here to say goodbye?"

She sighed and shook her head. "Still trying to get rid of me?"

"Still trying to keep you safe," he said.

Heat suffused his face as he added, "And… I haven't acted very professionally since you arrived. I'm sorry." He hoped she recognized that he was sincere. "I was taken by surprise."

"Why?"

"The mayor hasn't had any interest in these cold cases until he called me to meet with you a couple of days ago," he said.

She tilted her head and studied his face, as if debating whether or not he spoke the truth. The mayor had probably given her another story entirely. "He said you're the one who's reluctant to work them."

"You've seen the proof that he's wrong." He stepped back into the vault then, to where he'd left the evidence strewn across the table. She joined him, and instead of making the space feel smaller, she somehow made it seem brighter and more open. He pointed to the recent results from the state police lab. "I've been working the cases and getting nowhere."

"But now I'm here," she said. "And that note will help us. Thanks to Mrs. Watson showing you the guest log, we have suspects," she said, and her voice vibrated with determination. "I can get some DNA from them."

"Not without a warrant," he said. "And no judge is going to grant you one just on the basis of them staying at the B and B with you."

"I'll get it some other way then, without them knowing it. From something in their rooms, and I can run it against the killer's DNA recovered from the crime scenes."

"You'll break and enter and risk getting caught in the act to obtain evidence that would be inadmissible anyway?" he asked with frustration. Now he remembered why he'd wanted to work the investigation alone, so that nobody else could jeopardize it. "Is this how you've solved so many cases in the past? With illegal methods?"

"It's not illegal if they've thrown something out. I'll follow them around, I'll wait…"

He shook his head, rejecting the idea just as he had

when she'd mentioned it back at the B and B. "It's too dangerous."

"For whom?" she asked, her voice sharp with suspicion. "You? Your friends you want to protect?"

"For you," he said. "I thought your father was going to convince you to leave here—for your protection."

"If you're so convinced that the killer isn't someone you know, why are you so determined to get me to leave?" she asked. "Why are you so worried that I'm in danger?"

"You've been threatened," he reminded her, "in a note that anyone could have slipped beneath your door. You're in danger, and you know it."

And not only was she in danger but she posed a danger. To the killer...

That was why that note had been left for her.

But she also posed a danger to Hoge. Ever since the mayor had ordered him to meet her, something had shifted inside him, and he felt more vulnerable now than he had in years. She wasn't just opening up the past but also him, making him wish for something that he knew was too great a risk. Rolland Moore hadn't made a relationship work; there was no way that Hoge, given his past, could either.

Eve shivered, and it wasn't just because of the damp air in the basement of the police department. It was because of the sheriff's chilling words. "I do know I'm in danger," she said. "I'm no fool."

"Foolhardy," he remarked.

She shook her head. "Determined and forewarned. So I'll be careful. But I'm not leaving no matter how much you or my father try to convince me I should."

"Why?" he asked. "Why are you so stubborn about this case?"

"About this killer," she said. "He's already gotten away with too many murders."

"So you want to give him the chance to try to get away with yours?"

"He won't," she assured him. "And I don't want him to get away with any more. I want to stop him."

He sighed raggedly. "So do I."

"No matter who he might be?" she asked.

His chest expanded as he drew in a deep breath, as if bracing himself, and then he nodded. "No matter who he is, he's a killer."

"So let's find him," she said.

He nodded again, as if in agreement, but he didn't move away from the small table in the middle of the vault.

"He's not in here," she said.

"I wanted to look at the evidence again."

With her...he'd said earlier, but then she'd showed him that note instead. He was staring at the crime scene photos like he'd stared at that paper, in horror. Sensing that he needed comfort, she stepped closer to him. Unfortunately she was used to seeing images like this, but as a small-town sheriff, he was probably not.

"As many of these kinds of photos as I've seen, they still get to me," she admitted. Still haunted her...

"Then why do it?" he asked.

"So that there might be fewer," she said. "So that more of the real perpetrators are brought to justice."

He looked up from the pictures, then to focus on her face, and the way he stared at her, with something like wonder and admiration, had her pulse quickening. Or maybe it was just the small space.

No. Those bothered him. Not her. *He* bothered her, made her feel things she had no business feeling during an investigation. Or any other time…

He glanced back at the photos. "They shouldn't affect me anymore," he said. "I've looked at them so many times."

"Are these the only murders you've had to deal with?"

"In Cold Creek," he replied. "But I worked in Detroit after graduating from the police academy. I saw a lot of horrible things during my years there."

Eve wasn't that surprised. His experience explained why he was so good at questioning people like he'd been questioning her. "I can imagine what you must have seen."

He was back to staring at her again, rather than those photos. She didn't meet his gaze, but she could almost feel it on her face. "It's too bad that it's so easy for you to imagine the worst."

Was he talking about crimes? Or about her thinking he might have been the one who'd threatened her?

Regret tugged at her. Regret that she couldn't be more trusting. But she just wasn't like her father. She couldn't be eternally optimistic and forgiving. Not yet…

But maybe, if the killer was caught, if justice was finally served, she might be able to embrace her faith again and move forward, instead of being so focused on the past. She wasn't the only one, though.

The sheriff had gone back to staring at the photos, and the look on his face…

Maybe it was just because, as he'd said, he'd looked

at them so many times, but it seemed like he actually knew the victims. But he'd been so young when they'd died that even if he'd known them, it was doubtful he would have personally remembered them.

"Tell me what you know about them," she said.

He pointed toward the first photo. "Loretta James. During her summer break from her first year of college, she was working at the ice cream stand at the edge of town. It was the last place she was seen before she turned up here—in the woods—some weeks after she'd gone missing."

Her body, in the photo, was covered with dirt and leaves from the shallow grave in which she'd been buried.

Eve shivered again, as it was too easy for her to imagine the worst. From reading the case files, she knew what the young girl had endured. She had been raped and strangled, not with bare hands, but with some kind of weapon that had nearly severed her carotid artery.

"Amy Simpson," he said, pointing to the next picture. "She was babysitting for the summer. She had taken the little boy to the park. It was the last place she was seen alive. Like Loretta, her body wasn't found until several days after she'd gone missing. She'd been buried in the woods too."

"And what about the little boy?" she asked, panic squeezing her heart at the thought of the child. "What happened to him?" There had been no mention of witnesses in the case files. "Was he killed too?"

He shook his head. "No. He was found alive…in the park."

"Did anyone interview him?" she asked.

"He was too young to talk," the sheriff replied. "Too young to tell anyone what he witnessed."

"Then," she said. "But now…"

He shook his head. "He wasn't even three years old."

"So that's why the killer let him live," she said, speculating.

"Or maybe he thought he'd die where he left him…" His voice trailed off, gruff with emotion, but then he cleared his throat and continued. "Locked in the trunk of Amy's car."

"Oh, that poor little boy," she murmured with heartfelt sympathy for the child.

"That poor girl," the sheriff said as he stared down at her picture.

Despite the suit jacket she wore, goose bumps raised on Eve's arms, and she was tempted to wrap them around herself. Had the same man who'd done that… threatened her, as well?

"All those poor girls," he continued. "Mary Torreson was the last victim in Cold Creek. She worked at the bait shop in town after school. Like the others, she went missing from her place of employment." He looked away from the photos to focus on her face. "Places of employment that tourists to the area would visit."

"Or townspeople," she said. "They go to ice cream stands and the park and bait shops." She pointed at the photos now. "You've told me what happened to them and where. I already knew that. I want to know *who* they were, *who* they knew…"

And who their killer was.

She suspected that the sheriff knew if not all, at least some, of those answers.

Chapter Ten

Silence hung heavy in the SUV, making Hoge's shoulders sag slightly from the weight of it. He carried it alone since Eve kept trying to initiate conversation.

She cleared her throat and tried again. "I thought you were going to tell me more about them, but you've barely said two words since we left the police department."

He shook his head, but he couldn't shake off that heaviness. That darkness…

It enveloped him. Crushed him…beneath the weight of it. Even the sky had gone dark with swiftly moving clouds. A storm was moving in. In the distance thunder rumbled, echoing the rumblings inside his head. The rumblings of the past…

"Sheriff…" she murmured. Then she called his name, "Hogan…"

"Hoge," he automatically corrected her. His father had always called him that and with such affection that he preferred it to his full name.

"Where are you taking me?" she asked. "And should I be concerned?"

He glanced across the console at her then, at the paleness of her skin and the wideness of her bright eyes. She was scared. He'd scared her.

Shame and regret added to the burden he already carried. This was why he couldn't risk a relationship—he didn't want to hurt anyone. "I'm sorry," he said. "I know you don't entirely trust me."

"Do you blame me?" she asked.

He noticed that she had one hand inside her bag, probably wrapped around the can of pepper spray she'd mentioned carrying when she walked to the police department. "I told you when we left that I'd *show* you who they were," he said. "I'm bringing you to where they lived, to their families."

She expelled a shaky breath. "Oh…"

"I'm sorry," he said again. But this was hard for him. Harder than she knew…

Maybe he should tell her everything. But, as she'd said, he could barely get out more than a few words right now…after going through all that evidence again.

Now this…

In the vault, he'd started with the oldest case first. But now he worked backward. He stopped at Mary Torreson's house, the closest to town, just a mile from the bait shop where she'd worked, to which she'd ridden her bike after school. She'd been the most recent victim, but even then it had been more than two decades since her murder. The bait shop was gone now, replaced with a gas station that had a small refrigerator for live worms and some tackle hanging among the snacks.

Mary's room was the same, though. Her mother let them into the teal-painted bedroom that was preserved exactly as Mary had left it…with all her stuffed animals tucked in among the pillows and Polaroid pictures tacked to a corkboard above her desk.

Eve leaned over Mary's desk to peer at all the photographs. "Do you recognize anyone in these?" she asked. "Anyone stick out to you?"

Hoge shook his head.

"I can tell you who they are," Mary's mother said from where she sat on the foot of the bed, a stuffed animal clutched in her skinny arms. "So you're that lady scientist?"

Eve nodded.

"'Bout time we get somebody in Cold Creek who knows what they're doing," she said with a pointed glance at him. "Your daddy sure didn't. I thought you might be different, Hoge, with your fancy education and all those years in the big city…" She shook her head, as if disgusted with him.

"I'm sorry, Mrs. Torreson," he said. "I know how difficult this has been for you."

The woman, with her straggly gray hair, snorted. "No, you don't."

He flinched, but he didn't argue with her, not even as she continued with a barrage of insults.

"Mrs. Torreson." Eve was the one who interrupted her. "Can we borrow these photographs? I want to crossreference them with any we might find at the other girls' houses."

Mrs. Torreson snorted again. "You might find a couple of things at Amy Simpson's, but there's nothing left of Loretta James's. Her folks got rid of *everything* that reminded them of her."

Hoge flinched again and closed his eyes as pain jabbed his heart. When he opened them, he found Eve staring at him like she had Mary's photographs, like he was a piece of evidence for her to study.

If she only knew…

Maybe he should tell her, but he still didn't completely trust her. He wasn't sure if she really wanted nothing to do with the mayor's reporters, or if she was going to keep them apprised of the investigation despite Hoge's protests. And he didn't want everyone to know his horrible secret. So, even though he was tempted, he wouldn't share it with her.

But she was smart—so smart—that she might figure it out on her own.

Eve wasn't like her father not only because she wasn't as optimistic or forgiving. She wasn't like him because she wasn't as empathetic either. She'd never known anyone who was…until now, until she saw how Hogan Moore dealt with the victims' families.

Despite how Mrs. Torreson had berated him during their entire visit, he'd been incredibly patient with her. And when they left, he squeezed her hand and apologized. "I'm so sorry it's taking so long to find your daughter's killer."

"You haven't found him yet," the woman replied. She shook her head. "You haven't even found her necklace, the one I keep asking you about."

"What necklace?" Eve asked.

Mrs. Torreson grabbed one of the photographs from her hand. She pointed to her daughter and to a necklace dangling from her neck. It was too small for Eve to see well in the picture. She'd take another look, with her magnifying glass, later.

"I looked," Hoge said. "It's not in the evidence."

"You looked," she scoffed. "Just like you looked for her killer. Nobody's found either."

"We will," he promised. "We will find her killer."

"We're close," Eve added. So close that the man had slipped a note under the door to her room at the B and B.

The woman shook her head. "I won't hold my breath. Your daddy promised the same thing, but he was always too busy holding court in Cold Creek Café to ever really work the case. Seems you are very much your father's son."

Hoge flinched, like he had a couple of times earlier when the woman's comments must have struck a nerve. Clearly he loved his father like Eve loved hers. But had the former sheriff been deserving of that love?

Had he been a good man like her father was? Or had he been a lazy lawman? Or worse…

One who'd purposely covered up murders?

She'd wondered if Hoge would do the same, to protect a friend, but his promise to Mrs. Torreson sounded genuine to her. Too many people had made promises to Eve they hadn't honored, and her heart ached yet with pain and disillusionment. So, like Mrs. Torreson, she wasn't going to hold her breath.

Hoge must have, though, because he released a shaky one when they climbed back into his SUV.

"I see why you didn't want to do this," she remarked. "She was pretty tough on you."

He shrugged, but his broad shoulders remained slightly down, as if carrying a heavy burden. "Understandably so. She's been waiting a long time for justice."

"She's not the only one…" Eve murmured, thinking of the man who'd lost a decade of his life and his reputation.

He glanced at her and started up the ignition. "No, she's not. Let's talk to the others."

A short while later he pulled the SUV into the gravel drive of a modest ranch house. A woman with a heavily lined face opened the door to them. Mrs. Simpson was just a little more welcoming to them than Mrs. Torreson had been. But as Mrs. Torreson had warned, she didn't have a lot of her daughter's things left. Still, she obliged Eve's request for photos and pulled out some old albums.

Eve knelt on the thin rug beside the coffee table on which the older woman had dropped the books. She picked one up and began flipping through it while the sheriff just stood there. She glanced up at him. "Aren't you going to help?"

"He's seen all these before," Mrs. Simpson replied for him. "He's gone through these books a couple of times the past couple of years and even before that, with his daddy, when the sheriff would come by to see if there was anything he missed."

Eve had known that Hoge recently reran the evidence for DNA matches, but she hadn't realized he'd been out already to speak to the victims' families. Apparently he'd been following up on the investigation he'd started with his father.

"You can take them," Mrs. Simpson offered. "It's too hard for me to look at them, to see how…" Her voice cracked with emotion and tears rushed to her eyes.

Hoge moved then, sliding his arm around her shoulders to hold her as she wept. Eve's heart ached for the woman's pain; maybe she was more empathetic than she'd thought. Or maybe something about the sheriff was opening her up to feel more, to let down the walls she'd built around her battered heart.

Mrs. Simpson pulled away from Hoge and wrapped her arms around herself. "It's just hard. She was such a sweet girl. She loved watching that little boy too. At least he survived."

"What happened to him?" Eve asked.

Mrs. Simpson shrugged. "I don't know. The Jameses gave him up after that, like the baby was bad luck or something." She sighed. "Maybe he was…"

Hoge flinched, like he had from Mrs. Torreson's attacks. But Mrs. Simpson hadn't attacked him like the other mother; in fact, she was very sweet.

Eve shook her head. The sheriff was distracting her too much. She needed to focus on what Mrs. Simpson had said—because she couldn't make sense of it. "I don't understand. What did the little boy have to do with the James family?"

"He was Loretta's little boy," Mrs. Simpson said. "She'd had him just a couple months before she died. Amy babysat him. But after she was murdered, too, nobody wanted him."

"Somebody did," the sheriff replied. "I heard he was adopted."

"That's good," Mrs. Simpson said with a short nod. "Amy really loved that little boy. He was such a cute little thing." She picked up one of the albums from the table and flipped it open. "She took all kinds of pictures of him like he was hers." She held the open book out to Eve.

Eve looked at the pudgy toddler. He had chubby cheeks and a smile so bright that Eve smiled looking at him. "He doesn't look like bad luck," she said.

"No, the bad luck was all his," Mrs. Simpson said. "Losing his momma and then the other girl who loved him." She sighed. "Poor thing. I hope he got a good home."

Tears stung Eve's eyes and sympathy overwhelmed her. Sympathy for the child and sympathy for this grieving mother who cared more about the toddler than his own family must have since they hadn't wanted him.

"Poor kid," Eve murmured.

"Thanks for the albums," Hoge said, his voice gruff. "We'll bring them back after Ms. Collins has a chance to go through them."

Apparently he didn't intend to look at them again. He hadn't even glanced at the picture of the little boy. But then he'd seen it before. He'd seen all the evidence before.

And so had his father.

Was this killer that good that he'd left nothing behind to lead to him? Or was there something they had missed—something that Eve would find? There must be, or why would she have been warned away?

The sheriff helped her carry out the albums to the SUV. After putting them in a box in the back seat, he slid beneath the steering wheel.

"The Jameses now?" she asked.

He stiffened but nodded. "They won't have anything for you to look at," he warned her, just as Mrs. Torreson had. "I'm not sure they'll even want to talk to you."

He was right.

Less than an hour later, they stood on the front porch of a run-down cabin in the woods. While the sound of a TV rumbled through an open window, nobody answered their knock at the door.

Like Hoge's body had stiffened earlier with tension or dread, Eve's stiffened now with suspicion. "Hello!" she called through that open window. "Please answer your door. I'm here with the sheriff. We have some questions regarding your daughter's murder."

The TV volume increased. And Eve gasped with shock. "Why won't they talk to us?" she asked Hoge.

He just shrugged.

"I have some idea," she said. "Maybe a guilty conscience…"

Maybe the killer's very first victim—Loretta James—had been the most accessible. A family member. And the next victim had been the babysitter of that family member's offspring.

"We need to get in there," Eve told the sheriff. She knocked again, hammering so hard on the door that her knuckles hurt.

He caught her hand in his and pulled it away from the door. "You're going to injure yourself," he admonished her. "You need to calm down."

But she couldn't, not now when she felt like she was so close to a real lead. "Can't you force them to open up?"

He shook his head. "We don't have a warrant. We can't force him to talk to us. And even if you tried, you're not going to get any useful information that way. Rubber hoses are considered coercion."

She'd once teased him about using rubber hoses, but she didn't find it amusing that he tossed the accusation back at her. "So how do you get useful information, Sheriff?"

"You make the person want to talk to you, want to

confide in you," he said. "You're sympathetic. Understanding. Supportive. Not confrontational."

"Good cop only?"

He nodded. "My father was the good cop every time."

"But your father didn't solve these murders," she reminded him and felt a flash of guilt when he flinched again. "Maybe someone needs to be bad cop now and get…" She realized what he'd said earlier. "*Him*…talking. Who is he and how do you know there's only one person in there?" She couldn't see anything through the screen but the faint glare of the TV set.

"Mr. James is the only one left in Cold Creek. His wife and his son moved away years ago."

So if the killer was one of Loretta's family members, two male suspects had been in close proximity with her and her son's babysitter. Her father and her brother. She hated to think like that, to think of the worst of possibly innocent people, but too many of the cold case murders she'd closed had been committed by family members of the victims.

Eve moved off the porch to the side of the house, to where a garbage can stood near a side door. So many bags filled it that the cover wasn't tight. She noticed a discarded live bait carton. And Mr. James fished. Maybe he used to buy his bait from Mary Torreson.

"This is it," she said as hope surged through her. She needed more than that discarded bait container, though. She needed a discarded drink or…

But when she reached for the garbage can, a strong hand encircled her wrist. Her pulse leaped from the sheriff's touch. "You don't have a warrant," he said.

"It's garbage," she pointed out. "Discarded."

"On private property with a sign posted at the end of the drive for no trespassing," the sheriff reminded her.

"A sign you violated," another voice chimed in from behind the screen of the side door. "You're trespassing."

Eve peered through the screen at the old man on the other side of it. He wasn't standing, at least not upright. He leaned on the walker that he'd pushed toward the door. He looked very old and very frail even while he bristled with outrage.

He hurled curses at them, banishing them from his property with threats of calling the real police on them, the state troopers. "Everybody considered your old man a hero," the guy continued, his anger directed at Hoge now. "But some of us knew the truth. I know the truth."

A chill raced over Eve's flesh. What was he talking about? What did he mean?

Hoge was tense, like he'd been earlier, but he didn't argue with the man. He didn't defend his father. He just bowed his head and murmured, "We're sorry to have bothered you."

"You're not wanted around here," the man said. "You never were. Get off my property and don't ever come back!"

Hoge nodded and turned away from the door—from the man—and headed toward his SUV, leaving Eve standing there alone.

"Sir—"

"You, too," he told her. "Git!"

"But sir, I'm trying to solve your daughter's murder—"

He spit at the screen, but no droplets penetrated it, nothing Eve could use as DNA. "She thought she was so damn smart," he said. "But she killed herself—with the choices she made. No good. Just like her kid. No good…"

"Sir," she began, trying to reason with him.

"Go," he said. "Get out of here and get out of Cold Creek unless you wanna wind up like her and the others."

She shivered at the threat, the threat that was so like the one shoved beneath her door.

"Eve!" the sheriff called out to her as he held open the passenger door of the SUV.

She glanced back at the screen door, but the old man was gone now. He'd moved surprisingly fast with that walker. And the TV volume increased even more. But it didn't drown out the threat that rang yet in her ears.

Was he the one?

Had she just come face-to-face with a killer?

Chapter Eleven

This was why he hadn't wanted to do this, hadn't wanted to come here. Hoge was shaking in the driver's seat, shaking nearly as badly as Eve was shaking but for entirely different reasons.

"He threatened me," she said. "We need to get his DNA. We have to take something from that garbage."

He was already backing down the long gravel drive, but she reached for her door handle, as if ready to hop out and retrieve something.

"We can run it against the evidence," she persisted.

"It's already been run," he assured her as he steered onto the street and turned the SUV back toward town.

"What? How? You said you had no suspects' DNA to run against the killer's."

"We have the victims' DNA," he said. "His daughter's…"

Eve nodded. "Of course. We can check to see if there is a familial relationship between her and her killer."

"I checked," he said. "There isn't."

"Maybe he isn't her father," she said. "Maybe he's her stepfather—"

He shook his head.

"Or her mom had an affair…"

"You either automatically think the worst of everyone you meet, or you really want it to be him," he said.

He must have hit a nerve because she glared at him and defended herself, "He threatened me—just like the person who left that note."

"He warned you," he said. "He's worried that you're in danger." Because of the bad luck… Hoge tried not to be superstitious; he was too spiritual for that. But sometimes he wondered—and worried—if it was true.

She snorted like Mrs. Torreson had earlier—with derision. "He's not worried about anyone or anything but whatever show he's watching right now."

A smile tugged at Hoge's mouth. "He's drowning out the rest of the world."

"What world?" she asked. "He's all alone."

"It's his choice," Hoge reminded her. "In his pain, he pushed everyone away."

She glanced over at him then. "You sound like you're speaking from experience," she mused. "Is that why you go off alone to your cabin?"

A smile twitched at his lips. "I enjoy my cabin. Nature. My little retreat…" On a whim he turned the wheel, executing a U-turn in the middle of the road.

Eve grasped the armrest, or maybe she was reaching for the door handle again, and exclaimed, "What are you doing?"

"Showing you who *I* am," he murmured—because he couldn't bring himself to tell her, to tell her what only his father and a couple of others knew. He didn't want her looking at him with pity or worse…

"My cabin is just a short distance from here," he said.

"Your cabin?" she asked.

Clearly she had no interest in it, in him, just as Rolland Moore's wife had had no interest. Embarrassed that he'd wanted to show it to her, he said, "I should stop by and make sure I closed it up properly since I left abruptly when the mayor called."

"So did the mayor's brother," she said. "The one who was at the B and B too."

"Ted left before you checked in," he reminded her.

"He doesn't live here?"

He shook his head. "Ted moved away years ago. So did Paul. But Paul can't make a go of his political career anywhere else, so he keeps coming back. Guess being mayor of a Podunk town is better than nothing."

"Why did you come back?" she asked.

"My dad got sick," he said.

"I'm sorry," she said, and she reached across the console to briefly touch his forearm. Beneath the jacket and shirt he wore, his skin tingled slightly from even that brief contact.

There was more to Eve than her expertise and her focus on solving cases. She was a caring person as well, but for some reason she seemed to want to hide that side of herself. Hoge was curious about that, curious about her, and what had made her so suspicious of everyone. Her job?

"That must have been hard," she said with sympathy.

She would understand, because the one emotion she'd freely shown him—besides suspicion—was her love for her father.

"Harder on him," he said. "He was such a strong and healthy man until the cancer…" His voice cracked as emotion overwhelmed him. Seeing Rolland so weak, in so much pain…it had been devastating.

Her hand touched his arm again, her fingers squeezing slightly, comfortingly, before she pulled away. Maybe she'd experienced that tingling sensation, as well. Could she be as drawn to him as he was to her?

It would be better if she wasn't—then it would be easier for him to ignore his interest in her. He shouldn't have brought her here, but something had compelled him to make that U-turn.

Hoge turned the SUV into the narrow drive that led back to the cabin where he'd shared so many happy times with his father. "This was his place," he said. Maybe that was why he needed to stop here, to feel that closeness to his father. "*Is* his place. I swear I can feel his presence here yet—in all the memories."

"I thought you were bringing me here to show me who *you* are," she said.

So she had heard the silly thing he'd muttered, the silly notion he had. Why did he want her to know him? It wasn't like she was sticking around. With someone threatening her, she should be leaving town right now. But he knew she wasn't going to until she'd done everything she could to find the killer.

To solve the murders…

Murders that should have been solved years ago. He knew she thought the same as the families of the victims.

The SUV bounced along the rutted two-track driveway, and the things they'd collected in the back bounced across the seat and onto the floor. She glanced into the back seat before focusing on him and on the small log cabin that came into view when the trees cleared a bit.

"It sounds like you brought me here," she continued, "because you want me to know *him*. Your father. The former sheriff."

"I do," he admitted. "It bothers me that you think he didn't do everything he could to solve these murders. He did. He was just busy..."

"Raising you on his own," she finished for him when he trailed off.

She paid attention—to what he'd said and maybe also to what he hadn't. How much had she figured out about him? Everything?

Eve peered through the windshield at the small log cabin sitting in the shadows of the tall trees surrounding them. A porch spanned the front of it and wound around both sides to the back. "So this is where you spent a lot of time with your father?"

"Yes." Hogan released a long, ragged sigh, and for the first time since they'd started their investigation, some of the tension seemed to ease from his body.

And she understood. "This is where you come to relax."

"Yeah," he replied with a slight chuckle. "That's what you're supposed to do at a cabin."

She glanced toward the small wooden structure and shuddered slightly. "But..."

"You still can't get past no indoor plumbing?" he asked with a smile.

She shook her head.

And he chuckled again. "It's nature at its finest, its purest. God's country."

She'd heard his muttered prayers for patience, but for the first time she realized that the sheriff wasn't just as empathetic as her father, he was as spiritual too. She wished she were still that spiritual, that she could regain the faith she'd lost and not just in mankind. "You love it here," she observed.

And for some reason, he seemed to want her to like it too.

He opened the driver's door and stepped out of the SUV. But she didn't even reach for the handle. It wasn't that she didn't want to see the cabin, or that she didn't want to like it; it was that she didn't want to like the sheriff.

She had to stay focused now—on the murders, on the killer who'd already threatened her. She couldn't afford to be distracted now, not when she was so close. But she wasn't worried about her life being in danger. She was worried about her heart. It had already been broken too many times. By her mother...

And David and Mindy...

She'd thought she could trust them. She'd thought they'd loved her. But they'd hurt her.

So badly. She couldn't risk that kind of pain again.

But Hogan Moore was distracting...

And handsome.

And maybe as pure as he considered this cabin in the woods. But how? With everything he'd seen...

She suspected it was far more than he would ever admit, and maybe not just crime scenes in Detroit. What had he seen here in Cold Creek besides those old photo albums and pictures?

And how had it not affected him as much as it had her? He was still so empathetic and caring and not nearly as suspicious of everyone as she was.

Eve didn't feel pure anymore. She felt jaded and cynical and unable to trust anyone, especially here—in a town that might have protected a killer all these years.

Hoge's father would have been the most culpable in that.

She reluctantly pushed open the passenger door and stepped out onto the overly tall grass. The sheriff had walked across the porch to test the front door of the cabin. He didn't unlock it, though, just continued around the porch to the other side, presumably to check a back door.

Eve followed him, and as she stepped around to the back of the cabin, she suddenly understood his love of the place, of the purity. The current rushed in the river winding through the property so near to the back deck hanging off the cabin that she could feel the spray of the water. She sucked in a breath at the iciness of the drops that touched her face. "So that's why it's called Cold Creek..."

Hogan chuckled. "Yes. It's cold but beautiful..." He glanced at her then, as if he considered her the same.

Maybe she came across that way, as uncaring, focused...but she was afraid to let anyone see how much she really cared. She was afraid of getting hurt. Again. She wasn't the only one who'd experienced pain, though. Their visits to the families had proven that.

And Hoge...

So many times she'd caught him flinching in pain and she suspected it wasn't solely over the comments and the accusations that had been made against his father. But she addressed those first with a question. "You really believe your father did everything he could to solve these murders?"

"I know he did," he replied, his deep voice reverberating with absolute certainty.

"You loved him a lot," she said. And maybe because of that he was unable to see anything but perfection in the man. She understood that—all too well. She loved her father so much, too, but he was very deserving of her love and admiration. She wasn't sure about Hoge's dad.

"He was a really good man," he insisted. "A spiritual man."

"Is that where you get it?" she asked.

He raised a brow, as if questioning how she knew that.

"I've heard you praying," she said, "for patience. I pray for that too."

He reached out for her hand and rubbed his thumb across the knuckles she'd chafed on the Jameses' door. "Not too successfully…"

His touch warmed her skin from the chill of the spraying water. It warmed something in her heart too. She pulled her hand from his grasp as that fear coursed through her, fear of him getting too close to her heart.

His mouth pulled down into a slight frown. "My prayers aren't always answered either."

He must have prayed for his father, for his health to improve. And he'd been let down when the man had died. "But you keep praying?" she asked with curiosity.

Her father had…all those years…he'd never lost his faith while serving time for another man's crime. He had never faltered. Was Hoge the same?

He nodded. "It makes me feel closer to God."

"Sometimes He feels very far away to me," she admitted. But she wanted Him back, wanted back the faith she'd once had and never questioned. But now she spent so much time questioning everyone else, and not just suspects. She questioned whether anyone told her the truth anymore.

He gestured at the trees and the water. "Here? I feel Him here. I see Him here—in all the beauty."

"I thought you brought me here to get to know you and your father," she said with a slight smile. "Not Our Father…"

"You do know Him," he said, as a statement.

And her smile widened that even though she struggled, he'd recognized her faith. Maybe she wasn't floundering as badly as she'd thought. "My father is a minister," she said.

"You're a church kid then," he said.

She shook her head. "He wasn't always one. Not when I was growing up…" He hadn't been there when she was growing up, but she refrained from telling him that. She already felt too vulnerable right now, too close to the sheriff. He was getting to her, scaling those walls she'd built so long ago, and she couldn't risk that.

For so many reasons…

"But you were always the sheriff's son," she remarked, bringing the conversation back to where they'd started. "Even going out to investigate these cases with him. Is that why you wanted to solve them on your own?"

"I just want to solve them now—like I promised my father I would. Not solving them was his greatest regret," Hoge shared. He turned to lean on the deck railing again and stared down at the rushing water. "He felt like he'd failed the victims. All the victims…"

"The three," she said. "He only knew about three."

"There were more victims than the dead," Hoge said. "You should know that now after we talked to the family members."

She nodded. "Their lives were destroyed too."

"That's why Mr. James acted how he did," Hoge said. "He's in pain."

"He's still a suspect to me," she said. Until she got a sample of his DNA and confirmed it matched only his daughter's and not the killer's.

"Everybody is," Hoge replied, and he turned back and focused on her. "Even me?"

"You're too young to have been the killer," she said, as he'd pointed out to her before. But he could still be protecting the killer, maybe as his father had.

"I don't know who it is," he said, as if he'd read her mind—or maybe just all the suspicion on her face.

Despite the walls she'd built around herself, she couldn't hide all her emotions. At least not her suspicions. "We'll find out," she said. But then she had to ask, "Do you want to know?"

"Of course," he replied immediately, almost automatically.

And she wondered. "Are you sure?" she asked. "Chances are that it will be someone you know."

He shrugged. "You don't know that. Those women worked in places where tourists would be."

"And two of them had a connection through that child," she said. "We should see if we can unseal his adoption records, if we can talk to him."

"He was too young to remember anything," the sheriff maintained.

He was probably right. The three-year-old she'd babysat just over a decade ago had grown into a teenager who didn't even recognize her now. What were the chances that a toddler would remember anything from three decades ago? Slim to none.

"He wouldn't even be able to remember his mother," she murmured. "And I wonder who his father was. Nobody said."

He shrugged again. "Maybe she didn't know."

"Or she didn't want anyone else to know," she said. "Or maybe *he* didn't want anyone else to know. He could have been older or married."

"Even if he was, it doesn't mean he murdered her and then his son's babysitter, as well," Hoge pointed out. He stared at her face, his eyes narrowed as he studied her.

She shivered and knew it wasn't because of that spray coming off the river rushing below the deck. "What?"

"You're not what I thought you'd be," he said.

"What did you think I would be?"

"A scientist," he said. "Interested only in facts. Instead you're all about suspicion and supposition with very little based on fact."

She closed her eyes as shame rushed over her. She had changed during this investigation—*because* of this investigation. "I just want to find him."

"For justice?" he asked, but he sounded doubtful, like he knew she had another reason.

Her other reason had checked into the B and B and was probably waiting for her right now at the café. She glanced at her watch. "I'm supposed to meet my father," she said.

"He's staying?" Hogan asked.

She sighed. "Thanks to you, he's worried about my safety."

"And he knows you're too stubborn to leave Cold Creek like you should," Hogan said.

"Now you sound like Mr. James."

He flinched. "I'm not threatening you," he said. "I would never do that."

He wasn't, but something about him threatened her. He wasn't just scaling those walls she'd built around her emotions; he was threatening to knock them down. And if he did, she would have no defenses left—nothing to protect her from falling and getting her heart broken all over again.

Chapter Twelve

Hoge had insisted on walking her into the café, to make sure that she stayed safe and not just because as sheriff it was his job to serve and protect.

He cared about her, cared about how much she cared about justice. And he was curious too. He wanted to know more about her.

She obviously didn't feel the same. She hadn't been very interested in the cabin he'd showed her except for an instant. He'd thought they'd been having a moment, that she'd understood and even shared his connection to the cabin and to his faith. But then she'd focused again on the murders, on finding the killer.

He should be too.

But she was proving a distraction to him. She was as much of a puzzle as the murders. Because, like with them, he couldn't entirely figure out her motivation.

Her father stood up as they approached the table where he'd been sitting in front of the big window that looked on to the street. "Sheriff, I'm glad Eve invited you to join us for dinner."

Her face flushed bright pink with embarrassment, and Hoge chuckled and gave her up. "She didn't."

Bruce Collins chuckled too. "I'm sure it was an oversight on her part. I'd love for you to share a meal with us."

Hoge was tempted. He was drawn to her father. Something about the man—his sincerity and openness—reminded him of his own father. And he missed Rolland Moore so very much.

But he'd already spent too much time with Eve, so much that he might get used to spending time with her. And she would be leaving Cold Creek—if not at her father's urging to stay safe—at least when the killer was caught.

If he could be caught...

Was the killer the one who'd left that note for her? Or was that someone doing what she'd suspected Hoge of doing—protecting if not the killer then the memory of him or perhaps his or her memories of the victims?

The mayor wasn't the only one who'd initially been reluctant to revisit these cold cases. Mr. James was still reluctant—no, *determined*—to forget all of his family.

This was Eve's family, *her* father, extending the invitation to dinner. As tempted as he was to accept, Hoge knew he shouldn't intrude, so he shook his head. "I really need to check in at the office."

He'd left messages for the men who'd been at the boardinghouse the night Eve had checked into the place. He wanted to talk to them, find out if they'd seen anyone skulking around the hall outside her room. Unlike Eve, he struggled to suspect that one of them had actually slid the note under her door, but he needed to ask that as well, if one of them had taken it upon himself to warn her away from Cold Creek and why.

It wouldn't be the first time since becoming sheriff that he'd had to question someone he knew—not when he knew everyone in town. So he would do his job, as he'd vowed to when he'd run for office.

Before leaving Eve and her father, though, he made one more remark, or perhaps it was a request. "Please, make sure she isn't alone," he told Mr. Collins. "She needs to be extra careful."

"*She*'s right here," Eve pointed out to him. "And *she* can take care of herself."

Her father smiled at Hoge. "Thank you for being concerned. I am too. That's why I'm staying in Cold Creek."

"Good," Hoge said, for many reasons…one of which being that he would like to get to know the minister better. In getting to know him, he would get to know his daughter better, as well. Not that he was any more interested in Eve than she was him. He couldn't be— not when he knew it was best for him and for anyone he cared about—to stay single. He just wanted to keep her safe.

"Have a wonderful dinner," he told them before he turned and headed toward the door. He really wasn't hungry. His stomach churned at the thought of questioning the men for whom he'd left messages. They were all his father's friends, men he'd known his whole life, but he had no choice.

He had to learn as much as he could about that threat, just as he had to learn as much as he could about the cold cases. Bringing Eve along with him today to meet the victims' families had given him a fresh perspective. And he realized there might have been things he'd missed, things his father had missed.

So he hurried back to the police department, eager to check his messages and to take another look at the evidence. But he didn't find just a list of messages in his office. He found a man.

He forced himself to swallow rather than utter his groan of frustration. "Mayor…"

Paul Prentice was sitting at his desk, his feet up on the surface, while he flipped through the files Hoge had left out. Hoge had told Doreen it was all right to allow Eve back into their office area; he hadn't made that exception for the mayor, though. He would speak with her later—after he got rid of Prentice.

"What are you doing here?" he asked. Besides obviously snooping…

If Prentice hadn't come here to snoop, he would have summoned Hoge to his office as he had twice before. He didn't look guilty over being caught going through the files. Instead he just looked annoyed.

"I've been waiting for you," Prentice replied, his tone accusatory. "Where have you been?"

"Doing my job," Hoge replied. "And you?"

"This is my job too. I'm making sure that you are cooperating fully with my consultant," the mayor said. "It's going to look bad to the media if you're reluctant to work with her to solve these cases."

"That's what I've been doing today," Hoge said. "Working those cases with Ms. Collins."

The mayor jumped up then. "Why weren't the reporters included?"

"Because I told you I wouldn't let them be involved in an open investigation," Hoge reminded him.

"They're in the building too," Prentice said. "They're also waiting for you. To be brought up to speed."

He hadn't walked past either of the reporters in the reception area. So Hoge stepped back into the hall and peered around. "Where are they?"

The mayor shrugged. "They were here just a few minutes ago."

Hopefully they'd given up on waiting for Hoge and had left. But he wanted to make sure they were gone and that they hadn't snooped through any of his files like the mayor had.

"They're not welcome here," Hoge said. And he wanted to add that neither was Paul but that would just incite the mayor to be more intrusive than he was already being. "When we have anything to report, we'll let them know."

"So you've made no progress?" Prentice asked with a sigh and a shake of his head. "Hoge, this is disappointing."

"Ms. Collins has only been here a few days," Hoge reminded him. And she'd already been threatened and that had only happened because someone considered her a threat.

Who?

Who had slid the note beneath her door? He needed to find out—before that person made good on their threat.

"You look exhausted," her father remarked.

Eve glanced up from her plate to find him intently studying her face. She was aware that she probably had dark circles under her eyes from her sleepless nights. While she could take care of herself, and had for many years, she was grateful her father had decided to stay in Cold Creek. She suspected she would sleep a little easier knowing that he'd taken the room next to hers… unless that put him in danger, as well.

"Are you sure you can stay? The inmates need you—"

"You need me," he said. "And there is another person working with them now, helping me out."

And she had only him. He knew that she had cut everyone else out of her life. "But are you sure that you should stay?" she asked.

He reached across the table and squeezed her hand. "I would leave," he said. "If I thought I could talk you into leaving, but I know what these cold cases mean to you."

She lowered her voice to a whisper and murmured, "To us."

He shook his head. "I made my peace years ago, Evie. Whatever you discover, it will be justice for the victims. Not for me."

Of course he would think that, as he was always so selfless, so forgiving. If only she could find the peace that he had…

Maybe she would—once the killer was caught. Maybe then she could forgive…everyone…

"We talked to the victims' families today," she shared, her heart clenching with the pain she remembered on their faces, in their voices—pain the sheriff had echoed as if he'd felt every bit of it himself.

"That must have been difficult," her father said. "I wish I could have been there, could have offered some comfort." Like he offered the prisoners…

She nodded. "I wish you could have, too, but the

sheriff did—no matter how rough some of those people were on him. He was very patient, very understanding…" Her voice cracked.

"He's very empathetic then," her father remarked.

She shrugged. "I guess or…" It was almost as if he'd been one of the survivors himself. Maybe he was…since he'd lost his father. Maybe all the years of investigating those cold cases had claimed his father's life as much as the cancer had.

"What?" her father prodded her.

And she told him everything she'd learned about Sheriff Hogan Moore and his dad. No matter that he was a small-town lawman and she was a big-city scientist, they shared a bond with their love for their fathers and their faith.

"That explains it," her dad murmured.

"What?" she asked.

"I got the impression that Sheriff Moore was a man who'd experienced a lot of pain," he explained. "And perhaps not just his own, as empathetic as he is."

She released a shaky breath. "I guess I should be relieved that I don't feel things that deeply," she said.

Her father smiled. "You do," he said. "You just try to ignore your feelings. You try to hide from them."

She sighed. "I wasn't talking about my feelings," she said. "I don't feel other people's feelings."

Her father shook his head. "I don't believe that."

"I felt sorry for them," she admitted. "But I didn't feel their pain like the sheriff did."

"Not their pain," her father agreed. "But you were feeling his. You're empathetic to him."

She shook her head now. "No. He's just easy to read." She wished. She still felt that there was something else, some other reason that he'd wanted to work these cases alone.

"Then it's too bad he didn't join us for dinner," her father said. "I think I would enjoy getting to know him better."

"I'm not sure he would let you get to know him," she said.

"So you're not the only one who's closed off to protect herself?" her father asked.

He knew her so well. But that was because she could trust him. He wouldn't hurt her. She couldn't say the same of anyone else, especially when someone out there had threatened to do exactly that, to hurt her.

"I don't know," she said. "I really don't know the sheriff all that well."

"Seems like he'd be a good man to get to know better," her father remarked.

She narrowed her eyes and studied his face. "I hope you're not matchmaking. I would never stay in a place like this."

Once the murders here were solved there would be no reason for her to stay. And with the sheriff's job here in the town in which he'd grown up, he had no reason to leave.

"Seems like a nice place to me," her father remarked. But then he always saw the good in everything and everyone.

She shuddered. "I don't think it is—not with a killer having hidden here so many years. Or maybe he wasn't hidden at all. Maybe everybody knows who he is, and they're protecting him."

"You said the mayor accepted your offer to work the cases," her father reminded her. "And that the sheriff showed you the evidence, evidence that he'd recently rerun through the DNA databases himself."

"True…"

"But someone still threatened me," she reminded him.

Her father's brow furrowed—maybe with concern for her. But then he murmured, "I wonder if you're the only one in danger."

Alarm shot through her, making her heart pound madly. "Has someone threatened you?"

He shook his head. "Of course not. I'm not sure anyone even realizes who I am."

Her heart rate slowed and the tension eased from her body.

"No," her father continued, "I was thinking about the sheriff."

"What about him?" she asked.

"He's working the cases too," her father said. "So surely, whoever threatened you to back off would also threaten him."

Her body tensed again as she realized her father was right. The sheriff was working the cases, but nobody might have realized that until today, until they'd visited all the victims' families.

Now whoever had left her that note would know that she wasn't the only threat of the killer being discovered. Despite what the mayor and maybe the rest of the town had believed, Hogan Moore wanted the murderer found too.

So how would the killer threaten him? With a note? Or something scarier? Something more lethal?

Chapter Thirteen

Every one of the men from the B and B had sworn that they'd seen nothing, had done nothing, that they really couldn't care less about the DNA consultant coming to Cold Creek. And Hoge believed them.

But was he making a mistake?

Was he not being suspicious enough?

While he didn't want to live his life like Eve Collins, being skeptical of everyone, maybe he needed to be less trusting of the people he knew. Maybe he needed to seriously consider that one of them could be a killer.

The killer...

The one Hoge wanted caught even more than Eve Collins did. Or did he? She was certainly determined to find this killer. Maybe her motivation was just as she'd said, to prevent more murders. Or maybe, like him, she had another reason for wanting this killer caught.

Today had been exceptionally rough on him, and unlike her, he didn't have his father to talk to anymore. Rolland Moore would have understood more than anyone how hard this day had been—even when he'd subjected Hoge to days like this in the past, to the meetings, to looking through all those photo albums…

Hoge had left them locked in the SUV after dropping Eve at the café, which was probably a good thing since the mayor had been waiting for him. After concluding his phone calls with the men staying at the B and B, he'd walked back out to the SUV to carry in the boxes.

Maybe he should have asked a deputy to complete the task, but he wanted to look through those albums again without anyone watching him, like the victim's mother or Eve Collins. He had caught her studying him several times during the day. Just as he suspected she had a personal reason for her determination to find this killer, she probably suspected the same of him. She was observant, so she wouldn't have missed how affected he'd been.

Too affected.

He needed to focus on the real victims and on finding their killer. So after carrying all the boxes down to the basement, he unlocked the vault and transferred the albums to that table in the middle of the enclosed space. Careful to make certain the door stayed open, he placed one of the empty boxes in front of it.

Then he focused on the albums from Amy Simpson's mom and the collection of photographs from Mary Torreson's bedroom wall. He had nothing from Loretta James—at least nothing he could scrutinize like he did those pictures.

In several of her photographs, Mary wore the small necklace her mother had claimed was missing. Something about that necklace, with its little peace symbol pendant, drew Hoge's attention. He'd seen it before. Not a replica but this specific one. While there were probably millions of the same necklace out there, this one had a significant chip at the top of it, like something had struck it.

Where had he seen it before?

It wasn't in the evidence; he knew that. He'd gone over everything from all three cases too many times before to have missed the necklace. He'd even dug up the area where her body had been found and come up empty. But he knew he'd seen it before. Where?

On someone else? In one of the other photos?

Or maybe he just remembered it from those Polaroids on Mary's bedroom wall. That was where her mother had pointed it out to Hoge, after having previously pointed it out to Hoge's father, asking if they'd recovered it. Just as she'd kept all those stuffed animals and pictures as a shrine to her dead daughter, she wanted the necklace too. Keeping her daughter's memory alive through her possessions was her way of dealing with her loss, while the James family's way of dealing had been to erase every trace of Loretta from their lives—even her child.

He pushed thoughts of the James family from his mind for the moment, unlike Eve, who was probably still focused on Mr. James as her likeliest suspect. Hoge was actually surprised she wasn't back at the police station yet.

Maybe Mr. Collins had convinced her to take a break for the evening. Hoge probably should too. He hadn't even eaten yet. But his stomach was still churning from all the stress of the day. He wasn't going to be able to eat or to sleep. He could already hear the echo of the scream from his nightmares…

The ones he knew he would have tonight…if he slept.

No. It was better for him to stay busy, to stay focused on the cases. And on that necklace...

He laid out the photos from Mary's bulletin boards and studied the necklace again. It was so familiar to him. But maybe it was just from these photos. Nonetheless he picked up one of Amy Simpson's mother's albums and flipped it open. The first contained all her baby pictures. He replaced it for another with the year on it matching the year she died. These were the most recent photographs of Amy that there were—except for the crime scenes photos—and that there would ever be now.

She would smile no more for a camera, and neither would Mary Torreson. He didn't know if Loretta James had ever smiled like they had; he'd only seen the crime-scene pictures of her, which was incredibly sad for so many reasons.

Should he have shared the reasons with Eve? Maybe if he had, she would have shared hers with him. But he doubted it. She didn't trust him. Did she trust anyone but her father?

What had happened to her? Was she just that mistrusting because of all the horrendous crimes she'd investigated? Or had a bad experience made her unable to trust?

And why was Hoge so interested in her and in everything about her? She was not one of the cases he needed to solve—that he should have already solved so she wouldn't have had to come to town in the first place.

Eve was in danger. She'd known that before dinner, but during the entire meal with her father, every other customer in the café and all of the employees had stared at her. None had been smiling or welcoming. Did anyone want her here? Did anyone want her solving these cold cases?

Was everyone protecting a killer?

Even the sheriff?

Or was her father right—was Hogan Moore potentially in danger too? After dinner she'd insisted on going back to the sheriff's office. Her father had walked her to the building but he hadn't come inside with her. He said he trusted that the sheriff would make sure she got safely back to the B and B. But she wondered if he had another reason, if he was still uneasy around police departments.

But why would police departments bother him when prisons did not?

Maybe it was this case that bothered him. But then why was he here?

Because he knew she needed him...

She was beginning to worry that he wasn't the only person she needed. She'd already admitted to the sheriff that she needed him professionally. Now she wondered if she had another reason to need him, like maybe she was beginning to develop feelings for him. But, for her, one of those feelings would need to be trust before the other feelings could follow.

Was he worthy of her trust?

He'd seemed like a good man, a caring man, while they'd talked to the victims' families. But there had been something else in his demeanor, something that made her think he had a secret of his own.

What was it?

And would it keep him safe or put him in as much danger as she was in?

She walked through the foyer of the police department to the door that led back to the offices. She knew the code now that unlocked that door and entered it without even speaking to whatever dispatcher might have been on duty then.

She wanted to talk only to the sheriff, to make sure he was safe, because her father's concern for him had made her concerned. So she hurried down the hall to where light spilled out of the open door of his office. But when she peered inside, she found it empty. He wouldn't have left the light on and the door open if he was gone.

Where was he?

Restroom?

"He's in the basement," one of the deputies remarked as he passed her on his way down the hall. "Probably hiding out from the mayor."

She glanced at the man in surprise, mostly that he'd shared any information with her but also that Paul Prentice hadn't ordered Hoge to city hall instead. "The mayor was here?" she asked.

He nodded. "With some reporters."

She groaned and understood why Hoge would have chosen to hide out. Or maybe he'd gone to the basement to protect the evidence from their prying. Hopefully he didn't think she had anything to do with the mayor's media campaign. Wanting to make certain that he didn't, she asked the deputy, "Can you open the door to the basement for me?"

The young man studied her face for a moment before replying, "The sheriff usually doesn't like us letting anyone else in there, but since he's already down there…" He shrugged and headed toward the end of the hall and the door to the basement, Eve close behind him.

Unlike the sheriff, who'd been careful to not show her the code when he unlocked the door, the deputy made no attempt to shield the console when he pressed in the numbers. While she appreciated his letting her into the basement, concern flickered through her that someone else might have figured out the code due to the deputy's carelessness.

It wasn't her job to admonish him, though, so she just smiled when he opened the door for her. As she passed him, she murmured, "Thank you." When the door swung shut behind her, she shivered. The flickering fluorescent bulbs left the metal stairwell in shadows.

She grasped the handrail as she carefully descended the stairs. Each step brought her deeper into the cellar and into the cold and dampness. She shivered again at the temperature and at her feeling of unease.

Where was Hoge?

She couldn't see him. The door to the vault stood open, though, a box propped against it. Why hadn't he looked out? Why hadn't he noticed the sound of the basement door opening or the stairs creaking as she walked down them?

She reached into the bag dangling from her shoulder and felt around for the canister of pepper spray…just in case. Just in case her father was right and something had happened to Hoge.

But what and how?

He was the sheriff and this was the police department. Surely the killer wasn't so bold as to attack him here. Holding the canister tightly in her hand, she stepped through the door to the vault.

Hoge glanced up from his absorption in the albums

lying open across the table. Then he held up his hands. "Don't shoot…"

She expelled a shaky breath. "I didn't know if something had happened to you. You didn't react to the door opening or to me coming down the stairs."

He shook his head. "I didn't hear anything."

Maybe, even with the door open, the vault was soundproof. Or maybe he'd been too focused on those albums.

"What is it?" she asked. "Did you find something?"

"The necklace."

She furrowed her brow as she tried to remember what he was talking about. There had been no necklace in those evidence boxes, but Mary Torreson's mom had asked about one. "Where did you find it?"

"On Amy Simpson."

"There was no necklace among her effects."

"Here," he said as he pointed toward a page of one of the photo albums.

Eve stepped closer and peered at the picture. A peace emblem dangled from a chain around the young girl's neck. She shrugged. "Are you sure it's the same?"

"See that nick there?" he asked, his deep voice rumbling with excitement. "That's the same one."

Eve dropped the pepper spray inside her bag and pulled out her magnifying glass. She took it from its cloth pouch and held it against the picture. Amy's necklace definitely had a nick. Hoge slid one of Mary's photographs beneath the magnifying glass, and Eve gasped. "It's the same necklace, but what does it mean?"

She understood science, DNA, and the killer's DNA—whoever he was—had been found on all three victims in Cold Creek and the other victim in Pennsylvania. "Could Amy have given the necklace to Mary?" she asked. "Were they friends?"

"Cold Creek is a small town," Hoge said. "But Amy was in college when she died—just home for the summer babysitting. And Mary was still in high school. They were more than four years apart in age, so they wouldn't have gone to school together."

"And they lived far apart," she remembered. But then in a rural town like Cold Creek, everything seemed far apart. "So what does it mean that this same necklace was worn by two different victims two years apart? And what does it mean that Loretta James's son's babysitter was killed two years after his mother was killed? Was he the link between those two victims and the necklace the link between the last two?"

"The killer is the link," Hoge murmured.

She shook her head. "But they weren't victims chosen at random for him. He knew them somehow. He must have taken that necklace from Amy to give to Mary."

Hoge shrugged. "Maybe. Or maybe Amy's mother gave it to Mary for some reason. I don't know what this means."

"You were excited," she reminded him. "You know what this means. That we're close." They were close to identifying a suspect; she just knew it.

Unfortunately the killer didn't have to work to identify the threat to him; he knew that she was one threat. And Hoge was undoubtedly another. She was just about to tell him that he could be in danger as well when metal creaked as the vault door slammed shut, plunging them into total darkness.

Startled, a small scream slipped out of her. It reverberated throughout the vault, hurting her ears. But she was worried that was not all that was about to get hurt.

Chapter Fourteen

Hoge was awake, but that hadn't stopped his nightmare from coming, from the darkness and fear consuming him as a woman screamed. His blood chilled even as sweat broke out on his forehead and upper lip and trickled between his shoulder blades.

"I'm sorry," a soft voice murmured in the darkness.

Eve. Not her...

Not the woman who screamed in his nightmares. He wasn't back *there*, locked in *that*...

No. He was in the evidence vault, with Eve. "What happened?" he asked. She'd been closer to the door than he had, but he hadn't seen her close it.

"I don't know," she said. "Could it have blown shut?"

He shook his head, then remembered the all-encompassing darkness. "No. It's too heavy, and there's no wind in the basement. I had a box propped against it too." To protect him from this very thing happening... from getting shut inside.

How had this happened? He hadn't noticed any movement outside the door, but he hadn't noticed any earlier, when she'd come down the stairs and stepped into the vault. He'd been too distracted. He listened now, trying to hear any noise outside the vault, but the walls were too thick, too soundproof. He uttered a ragged sigh even as panic pressed on his lungs, making it hard for him to breathe easily.

"Are you okay?" she asked.

"Yeah..." But the lie nearly stuck in his throat, which felt as if it was closing up.

"So you know how to get out of here?" she asked. "There's a way to open the door from the inside?"

That pressure on his chest increased, squeezing his lungs so that he could barely draw a breath. "No..."

"What do you mean?" she asked.

"We're locked inside." His worst nightmare. The darkness, the enclosed space...

But then a light flickered on, burning a small hole in the darkness. The glow from Eve's cell phone illuminated the space, but many dark shadows remained, making the vault seem even smaller—the walls closer. He gasped, trying to draw in some air.

"You're not okay. I'll get us out of here" she said as she punched in a number on the phone. He knew what she'd find out before she murmured, "I can't get a signal."

As well as too close, the walls were too thick. "You won't get one in here," he said. "We're trapped." And that panic pressed even harder on his lungs. His head getting light from lack of oxygen or anxiety, he swayed and nearly fell onto the table. The wooden legs scratched across the metal floor of the vault.

The light bounced as Eve grabbed for him, her small

hands grasping his arms as if she was trying to hold him up. "Sit down," she said.

There was no place to sit but the floor. So that he wouldn't wind up sprawled across it, he gripped the edge of the table to steady himself. He was tempted to grip her instead, to hang on to her for comfort, like he used to hang on to his dad when he was little and in the throes of one of his nightmares.

But he wasn't a little boy anymore. He was the sheriff. And he had to get a grip. He forced himself to draw a deep breath, and after releasing it, he said, "I'm fine."

"No, you're not," she said. "You're panicking that we're trapped."

Trapped...

That feeling raced over him again, making him shudder.

"But we're not," she said. "Somebody will let us out soon."

"Who?" he asked. Whoever had closed that door on them certainly had no intention of letting them out again...at least not until their oxygen ran out.

"The deputy who unlocked the basement door for me," she said. "I'm sure he'll check on us."

"Unless he gets sent out on a call..."

"Then my father will check on us," she said. "He's waiting for me at the B and B, so he'll come here if I don't show up there."

"When?" he asked.

Before their oxygen ran out...? How much did the vault hold? The heavy steel structure wasn't small, but it was so enclosed that no air could get in unless the door was open. How long would they be able to breathe? Days...or hours?

* * *

Maybe Eve was more empathetic than she'd thought because she could feel the sheriff's panic as surely as if it was her own. Or maybe it was?

"My father won't wait long," she said. "He'll come looking for me. *Soon*." Was she trying to convince Hogan Moore or herself? No. She was confident. Her father would make certain he found her if he had to search everywhere in Cold Creek. They'd been separated too many years for him to give up on her…like she'd once given up on him. But then she hadn't known the truth. Only the lies her mother had told, that he'd abandoned them…

"Yes, he will," the sheriff said, his voice deep and assured again.

He must have noticed that she was beginning to panic, too, and wanted to soothe her fears—because he didn't know her father. He didn't know how wonderful a man Bruce Collins was.

Just as some other police officers, a prosecutor, a judge and a jury hadn't realized it either so many years ago. While their error had been corrected, he hadn't been entirely cleared, and he wouldn't be until the real killer was brought to justice.

"How—how do you think we got shut in here?" she asked. "Who would have closed the door on us?"

"I don't know," the sheriff replied. "Maybe it was an accident and nobody realized we were inside."

But they'd been talking. Could someone have not heard them? Or was that why someone had closed them inside—because he *had* heard them?

He knew they'd figured out the victims were connected somehow. But then that meant the killer had access to the police department and to the evidence room. As careless as the deputy had been, she could imagine it hadn't been that hard for the person to get inside the police department or the cellar.

"Do you really believe we were accidentally shut inside here?" she asked.

"I don't know what to believe anymore," he said. "I really wanted to think that the killer was just some stranger who'd passed through Cold Creek a few times."

"You realize now that it's somebody you could know—maybe quite well."

In the glow of her cell screen, he shook his head. "No. I might know the person but obviously not very well."

"Some people can hide their dark sides," she said. "Often their own family members don't even know how dangerous they are." Or in the case of her mother and father, how *not* dangerous they were.

"Are you speaking from experience?" he asked.

She tensed. He was more observant than was comfortable for her. "What do you mean?"

"Do you have a dark side?"

She sighed. "No. But I've been in the dark before tonight."

"Me too," the sheriff murmured. And he seemed to sway slightly again.

Eve reached for him, sliding her arm around his back. "Come on. Sit on the floor before you fall on it."

He didn't argue this time. Using the edge of the table, he lowered himself to the ground and away from Eve's touch. Uncomfortable standing while he sat, she followed him down. "Are you okay?" she asked.

"Probably just hungry again," he said.

They'd been together most of the day, and she hadn't seen him eat. He hadn't joined them for dinner at the café. Leaving her cell sitting on the floor, the screen illuminated, she fumbled around inside her bag until she came out with a couple granola bars and a couple of juice boxes.

"What else do you have in that thing?" he asked. "Any power tools we can use to cut our way out?"

She chuckled. "This thing's already too heavy," she said. "But after this, I might consider it."

"Hopefully you'll never get shut in an enclosed space like this again." He shuddered.

"Is that what happened to you?" she asked. "You accidentally get shut in a fridge or a closet when you were younger?"

"Something like that," he murmured.

She tensed now. "Your father wasn't abusive, was he?"

"Never," he replied quickly—almost too quickly. "He was a wonderful man. You would've thought so, too, had you met him."

She wasn't so sure.

He must have sensed that reaction of hers as well because he said, "Your father reminds me of him—very warm and welcoming."

"Somebody in this town was warm and welcoming?" she asked with feigned shock.

He laughed. Talking with her must have eased some of his tension. Almost absentmindedly, he ripped open the package and took a bite of the granola bar. Then he grimaced.

"What's wrong?" she asked.

"How long was this thing in your bag?" he asked.

"The way I go through them, it couldn't have been long," she admitted. She ripped open another and took a bite. "Mine's fine." She held it out to him. "Want the rest of it?"

He shook his head. "No thanks. I appreciate you sharing, though." He glanced around as if looking for somewhere to pitch the bar he'd bitten.

She held out her hand for it. "I'll put it back in my bag and throw it out later," she offered.

He passed it over to her. When his fingers brushed hers, an odd sensation raced over her skin. She shivered. "Are you cold?" he asked.

Before she could even answer, he shrugged off his jacket and wrapped it around her shoulders. She would have protested…if it weren't so warm and somehow comforting.

Not that long ago he had seemed to be the one who'd needed comforting. But now he offered it to her. Another trait he had in common with her father.

If Hoge was at all like the former sheriff, it made sense that her father reminded him of his own dad. Maybe they really were alike. So maybe if she told him what had happened, he would understand. Maybe he would be as determined as she was to find the killer.

If they ever got out of here…

Despite the warmth of his jacket, she shivered.

"You're still cold," he said, and he slid his arm around her shoulders, tucking her close to his side.

"Aren't you?" she asked. "You shouldn't have given me your jacket."

"I'm fine," he told her. "I'm actually warm."

He was. Even through his jacket and her suit coat, his warmth penetrated, and something bloomed inside her, spreading throughout her chest—to her heart. She turned her head and studied his profile. His jaw was square and strong, his nose had a slight indent to it, as if it had been broken before, and his lips…

They were pressed in a tight line. Despite his taking care of her, he was still tense with dread.

"My father will find us," she promised. And to reassure him, she reached up to touch his cheek. He turned his head and his lips brushed across her fingertips.

Her breath caught. She was more scared of this than of nobody finding them in the vault. She jerked her hand back, but before she could pull away from him, he leaned closer.

His lips touched her cheek. "Thank you," he murmured.

"For what?" she asked. "A stale granola bar?"

"For making being locked in the dark not so very scary anymore…"

Anymore.

He definitely had phobias that haunted him. She had them as well, the fear of falling in love. And she was so afraid that she was about to…despite her mistrust and fear of being hurt again.

But he seemed like such a good man, such a faithful man. She'd thought the same of her fiancé once, too, though, and she'd been deceived.

But Hoge wasn't her fiancé. Was it fair that she judged him the same when he'd shown her nothing but his empathy and dedication today?

She was the one who leaned in now, but instead of brushing her lips across his cheek, she brushed them across his mouth. He gasped.

At her audaciousness? Or something else…

The rattling noise she heard too? Someone was outside the vault. Was he trying to get them out? Or making certain that they would *never* get out?

Chapter Fifteen

Sunlight streamed through Hoge's blinds, shining in his face before he even opened his eyes. When he did and found himself lying in his bed in his bedroom in his house, he offered up a heartfelt prayer of thanks and a sigh of relief that Eve Collins had been right.

"Thank you, God," he murmured. "Thank you for sending Bruce Collins." The man truly was a minister of God.

Her father, with Doreen's help, had found them last night. When Eve hadn't returned to the B and B, Mr. Collins had come to the police department in search of them. As Hoge had suspected, the deputy had been out on a call—those teenagers again sneaking out after their parents had grounded them. So the deputy hadn't realized he and Eve hadn't come up from the basement... until Doreen had put out a call asking if anyone had seen Eve or the sheriff that evening.

The deputy had radioed back to the dispatcher where he'd seen them last and Doreen had brought Mr. Collins down to the basement to help her look for them. When she hadn't seen them, she'd started back up the steps.

Mr. Collins had stopped her and asked her to search inside the vault.

If he hadn't...

Would they have been found in time?

Despite the warmth of the blankets covering him, Hoge shivered at the thought.

He wasn't sure how much oxygen they'd had inside the vault. He only knew that all the air had left his lungs when Eve had kissed him. And for a moment his nightmare had become a dream come true...

A dream he hadn't even realized he'd had, of Eve kissing him. Caring for him...

She'd been so sweet and comforting when he'd devolved into his mass of phobias.

But that kiss had given him another fear...that he was falling for a woman who was in extreme danger. The only thing that would make that worse would be if he was the one who had somehow put her in danger. Or if he was the danger.

That was something he wasn't going to think about now, though. Or ever...

Just as he was never going to risk it. They were already in too much peril.

Which one of them was the reason that the door had been closed? Or was it both of them?

Instead of protecting Eve, Hoge had been so distracted that someone had gotten close enough to her—to *them*—to trap them inside the vault.

Hoge had gotten close to her, too, so close that he could almost smell that cinnamony scent of hers. Or was it clinging yet to his jacket that he'd slung over the back of a chair next to the bed?

She'd felt so good in his arms, so right...

But being attracted to her was distracting him and might cost them both their lives. He needed to focus fully on finding the killer—before he made another attempt on either of their lives.

Hoge was beginning to believe her—that the killer was in Cold Creek, that maybe he had always been in Cold Creek. Or if the killer had died, then someone else was intent on protecting him or protecting themselves from the stigma of being either related or involved with a killer.

But how had that person gained access not just to the sheriff's office but also to the basement? Eve had remarked, after they'd been released from the vault, that she knew the code to the door from how the deputy had punched in the numbers when he opened it for her.

Had someone else picked up on the code the same way? Perhaps the mayor, who'd been hanging around the police department earlier that day? Or even the reporters he'd brought with him, whom Hoge had never seen.

Maybe they'd already been in the basement, trying to access the evidence for their reports. But why shut him and Eve inside the vault…

Unless one of them had a connection to the killer.

The person threatening Eve didn't have to be male—if they were only protecting someone they knew, someone whose crimes they didn't want revealed. Anyone could have slipped that note under her door.

And it could have been almost anyone who'd closed that vault door and locked them inside…anyone with access to the police department.

Had the intention been to scare them away from their investigation?

Or to kill them?

And having failed, would they try again?

I'll be fine...

That was what Eve had told her father before she'd left for her meeting at city hall. The mayor had sent for her that morning, his call awakening her after she'd finally fallen asleep. She'd like to think it was the ordeal the night before that had kept her awake. That getting locked in the vault had scared her so much that she hadn't been able to rest.

But she knew what had really scared her had been that kiss...

Why had she kissed him?

She'd been keeping secrets from the sheriff so he wouldn't think she was unprofessional, but then she'd kissed him. What had she been thinking?

She hadn't been thinking. For the first time in a long time she'd been feeling—some strange attraction that she hadn't felt for years...if ever. Had she ever been as intrigued, as drawn to a man as she was Hogan Moore? No. Not even her ex-fiancé had affected her like Hoge did.

But her ex-fiancé—and her former best friend—had proved how painful it was to trust the wrong people. Mindy had told Eve over and over again how blessed she was to have David. But then Eve had walked into David's apartment and caught them...

Heat rushed through her with the embarrassment and anger she'd felt then. Just twenty, she'd been so young and naive to believe either of them had ever cared about her. Her own mother hadn't even cared about her, or she would have told her the truth about her father instead of those hateful lies. Eve wouldn't make the mistake of trusting anyone again.

Hoge wasn't professing his love, anyway. He'd only kissed her cheek, probably to comfort her. When she'd touched her lips to his, he hadn't even kissed her back.

Of course, he hadn't had time before the door had opened to her father and Doreen. Her face heated at that memory, at the embarrassment and twinge of regret she'd felt before relief had rushed over her.

Just as she'd promised the sheriff, her father had found them. But who could have shut that door on them?

The mayor?

The deputy who'd let her into the basement had said he was there shortly before her.

And now, here she was, about to walk into the office of the man who could have locked her and Hoge inside that vault. But that wasn't the only thing he might have done.

He was old enough when those first murders had been committed to be the killer. And Hoge had mentioned something about his leaving town before and having to return.

Why?

Because he'd been worried someone might connect him to other crimes?

Despite what the mayor claimed to everyone else, he hadn't sought her out. In fact he hadn't accepted her offer to work the cold cases until she'd made it pretty clear that she was going to investigate no matter what, and that the media might be interested to learn the mayor was reluctant to have the murders of three young women solved. Once she'd mentioned the media, he'd jumped on her offer.

That had been a mistake, though, because now he was trying to force reporters into her and Hoge's investigation. Was that because he wanted the media coverage? Or because he wanted to stay apprised of the investigation, so he'd know when they were close to identifying a suspect?

"Ms. Collins?" Alice called out to her. "Are you all right?"

No. She wasn't. But she forced herself to smile at the woman who, despite her pretty white hair, had nearly no lines on her face. "I'm fine," she assured the receptionist.

The older woman studied her as if she debated Eve's claim, but she was too polite to argue. All she did was prod her with the reminder, "The mayor is waiting for you. You can let yourself into his office."

She wasn't sure she wanted to go inside, that she wanted to see him at all, not with all the suspicions swirling around her mind.

At least the woman was out here, at least Eve would be safe…unless there was another way out of his office. It was big enough that it probably had another entrance or two.

While she grasped the doorknob with one hand, she reached inside her bag with the other. She was looking for her canister of pepper spray, but she touched several other things first. The cloth bag from her magnifying glass. Her wallet. The torn packaging of a granola bar with only one bite out of it—she'd forgotten to throw it out. A small smile curved her lips.

She moved her hand and encountered her phone next. Maybe she should call him. Maybe she should let him know about this meeting despite the mayor's order for her to keep it just between her and him.

Why didn't he want Hoge here?

Because he'd included the reporters again?

Because he was going to force them into this investigation despite Hoge's protests?

Hoge wasn't the only one protesting their interference. She'd made that clear to Paul Prentice. Maybe he thought he could get her to change her mind, though.

Not that she would…

About the reporters.

Or about someone in this town being the killer or trying to protect the killer.

Was the mayor that someone?

Finally her fingers closed around the cold metal of the canister of pepper spray.

She wasn't sure why the mayor had called her here— why he wanted to get her alone without the sheriff. But she wasn't taking any chances with her safety—not after last night.

She'd taken the biggest risk last night—not when she'd been locked inside the vault but when she'd kissed the sheriff. Then she had risked her heart.

Now she could be risking her life…

Chapter Sixteen

She hadn't been waiting for him at the police department—not in his office—nor in the hallway or even in the basement. Checking the cellar, and the vault, had brought back all his fears and phobias but most of all his concern for Eve's safety. And so he'd headed to the B and B but he found only one Collins sitting in the kitchen eating cranberry orange muffins with Pam Watson.

"Sheriff," Mr. Collins greeted him with that welcoming smile he'd mentioned to Eve.

"Hoge," he corrected the man. "Please, call me Hoge."

"Short for Hogan?"

He nodded.

"Unique and strong," he remarked with a head bob. "I like it."

Hoge liked Mr. Collins. "I wasn't very strong last night," he admitted ruefully.

"Why do you say that?" Mr. Collins asked.

"I couldn't get Eve and myself out of the vault," he explained. "I'm so grateful that you did."

"Ms. Bevaas did everything," Mr. Collins said.

Hoge's brow furrowed with confusion until he remembered Doreen's last name. Had she really been so formal with the consultant's dad when she always insisted that everyone else call her Doreen?

Maybe Eve was right. Maybe nobody was being that welcoming to her or even to her father.

Except for the B and B owner who poured more coffee into the mug in front of her guest. "Mr. Collins was so concerned last night about you both," Pam said. "Sounds like he had good cause to be. Did someone really shut you inside the vault?"

That was what Hoge believed, but not wanting to spread rumors and conjecture, he shrugged. "The door probably just swung shut on its own. That thing is so old."

Pam nodded as if in agreement, although she'd never seen it—that he knew of...

Maybe he was getting as suspicious of everyone as Eve was. But maybe he needed to be—if he was ever going to solve these cold cases.

"I should get to making the beds," she said. But before she headed out of the kitchen, she set a cup of coffee and a plate of the cranberry orange muffins on the counter in front of him.

"Thanks," he said with an appreciative smile and a twinge of guilt for even entertaining suspicious thoughts about her. She was a sweet and honest woman.

Once she'd left the room, Mr. Collins turned toward him and said, "You don't believe that door closed on its own and accidentally shut you and Eve in the vault. You don't believe that any more than Eve or I do."

Hoge glanced around the kitchen, which was empty

now but for the two of them. "Where is Eve? Is she still sleeping?"

Miraculously he'd managed a few hours of sleep without any nightmares.

"The mayor called her for a meeting this morning," her father replied. "You weren't included?"

Hoge shook his head. "No…" Not that he'd been included in every meeting they'd had, but something about being excluded from this one made him uneasy. "Do you know what it's about?"

Her dad shook his head. "No. And neither did Eve from the voice mail he left her."

A chill zipped down Hoge's spine, and he shivered. Why would the mayor want to meet her alone—after last night? Was he looking for another opportunity to intimidate her? Or worse?

"You don't trust the man," Bruce Collins said with the certainty of someone who trusted his own observations and instincts.

Hoge's father had been like that too. But had he trusted someone he shouldn't have?

If Eve was right, and the killer was someone Hoge knew, then Rolland Moore had known him too…known him even longer and therefore better.

"No, I don't trust Paul Prentice," Hoge admitted. His father hadn't either. They'd never been close like Rolland had been to Uncle Ted. Maybe that was why Paul resented Rolland so much—because Hoge's father had had the relationship with his big brother that Paul wanted.

Or maybe Paul had another reason for disliking his father? Because he'd feared that he might discover Paul was a killer…

Leaving the muffins and coffee untouched, Hoge jumped up from the stool he'd taken next to Mr. Collins. "I don't want Eve to be alone with him."

It didn't matter that he'd not been invited to this meeting. Hoge intended to crash it—to make sure that Eve was safe.

The mayor was alone in his office when Eve let herself in the door, as his receptionist had directed her to. She would have actually been happy had he included reporters in this meeting. But for some reason he'd really wanted to meet her alone.

So much so that after she stepped over the threshold into his cavernous office, he walked behind her and locked the door. Locking her inside with him?

Or locking someone else out?

Hoge.

He really didn't want him at this meeting.

"I've been waiting for you," he said with his usual impatience.

"Why?" she asked.

"Because you're late," he patronizingly replied, as if she were an idiot.

She bristled with anger and with suspicion. The killer who'd raped and murdered those girls obviously didn't respect women either. But it wasn't just women the mayor didn't respect. From all the disparaging remarks Paul Prentice had made about the sheriff, he clearly didn't respect Hoge either.

"I didn't play your voice mail right away," she admitted. Although his call had awakened her, she hadn't answered it, and she had delayed playing his message because she had not wanted to deal with him after last night. She already had too much else to deal with...

Like being locked up in an evidence vault...

And kissing the sheriff.

"I heard about what happened last night," he said.

Heard about? Or witnessed?

Had he been there, standing outside the door he'd closed on her and Hoge?

"How did you hear?" she asked.

He shrugged, but his face flushed slightly. "Small towns are rife with gossip."

Eve wouldn't know. Nobody would talk to her, let alone gossip with her. "Well, it really happened," she said.

"That place is ancient, literally," Paul Prentice said. "I'm not surprised someone got accidentally shut inside that old vault."

Was he not surprised because he'd been there? Because he'd closed the door on them?

"I don't believe it was an accident," she said. She'd spent time in that vault earlier in the week and the door hadn't closed on her and there hadn't even been a box propped against it then. She shuddered at the thought that she could have been locked inside alone.

She might have developed her own phobias of enclosed places after that. But now she'd developed another fear entirely—the fear of falling in love again.

Or maybe for the first time...because she'd never been as drawn to David as she was to Hoge. Of course she'd been young then; she hadn't known what real love was. Only betrayal...

"What else could it have been but an accident?" the

mayor asked. "It's not like somebody would purposely shut you inside that thing."

Maybe she should have cleared it with Hoge first, but she found herself telling the mayor about the threatening note she'd received at the B and B.

Instead of expressing any concern for her, the mayor snorted.

"You don't believe me?" she asked, and now she was truly offended. She didn't lie—not when she knew all too well the pain that lies could cause.

She felt a twinge of guilt now—she also hadn't been completely honest with the sheriff. He'd asked her several times what her interest was in these cold cases, and she hadn't told him the whole truth. Sure, she didn't want the killer to hurt anyone else. And she wanted justice for the victims.

But she also wanted vindication too.

"I believe someone put that note under your door," the mayor assured her. "But I don't think it was the killer."

"The sheriff told me you believe someone passing through town committed the murders."

He shrugged. "That was what I once thought. But I don't believe that anymore," he said. "I figured out who the killer is—or *was*—actually."

A pang of regret struck Eve before she reminded herself that she didn't trust the mayor. A dead killer made his town safe and, therefore, much more marketable.

"Really?" she asked. "Who?"

"The sheriff."

She shook her head. "Hoge would have been a baby when that first murder happened. And a toddler when the second happened." Probably no older than Loretta James's now abandoned baby had been.

"Obviously I'm not talking about Hoge," the mayor said in that condescending tone that grated on Eve's nerves. "I'm talking about the man who will always be remembered as the sheriff because he held his job longer than anyone else—despite never solving those murders."

"Hoge's father."

He nodded. "Rolland Moore. He was definitely old enough to have committed those murders and more of them."

She shivered at the thought of Hoge's father being a killer. She knew what that felt like to consider, for even a moment, that the person you loved most was a monster. But she shook her head, shaking off that horrific thought. "A living person wrote that note—"

"Hoge," Prentice said. "Hoge would do anything to protect his father's memory. He still idolizes that man."

She couldn't argue that. Hoge clearly thought the world of his father. "Hoge didn't lock us in that vault," she said.

He sneered. "Nobody locked you in that vault—"

"Obviously the door is too heavy to have closed on its own," she said—with the same condescending tone he'd been using with her. "And there was also a box propped in front of it."

His eyes narrowed and he stared intensely at her, as his face flushed with anger. He didn't like being treated the way he treated others.

To stem off his next argument, she continued, "And there is no way Hoge could have closed that door on us without me noticing. I was standing between him and the door."

Like the mayor stood between her and the door now. She trusted him even less as he tried passing off blame on to everyone else.

"And there's no way he would have shut himself inside anyway," she insisted.

"Because of his claustrophobia?" The mayor smirked. "Everybody knows about that. Maybe one of his deputies locked him inside as a joke."

"I doubt any of them would be that cruel," she said. As cruel as the mayor was being to laugh about someone else's fears.

The mayor's smirk widened even more. "Nobody likes Hoge. They don't think he deserved to just step in and take over as sheriff just because his dad was."

"He was elected to office," she reminded the mayor. "Just like you, people voted for him."

His flush deepened to an even darker shade of red. "Maybe some people did—out of some kind of misplaced loyalty to his dad. But none of Hoge's people are as loyal to him."

Was that because one or more of them spied on him for the mayor? How else would Paul Prentice have known about them getting locked inside the vault—unless he'd been the one who'd locked them inside?

"And nobody's as loyal to the old sheriff as his son is," the mayor continued. "He would do anything to make sure that his father isn't revealed to be the killer. So you should be careful around him."

She'd been trapped with him and he'd done nothing to harm her…but make her start falling for him.

"Especially when you take his DNA," the mayor concluded.

She stared at him for a moment before asking, "Whose? Rolland Moore has been dead a couple of years." Did the mayor want her to dig up his body? She wouldn't put it past him.

"Hoge's," he said. "His DNA will prove that he's related to the killer, right? With Hoge's DNA, you'll be able to prove that his father is the killer."

"I can build family trees with DNA," she admitted. That was how she'd tracked down previous killers.

"Then take Hoge's DNA," the mayor urged. "It'll prove what I'm telling you."

His quickness to assign the blame to a dead man gave her pause.

"Or are you afraid to learn the truth?" he asked. "I thought that's why you're here."

"It is," she said.

But she didn't need to take Hoge's DNA to prove it. She already had some on the granola bar in her purse. His wasn't the only DNA she wanted to run against the killer's, though.

The door rattled suddenly, as someone tried to turn the knob. Instead of looking at it, like the mayor did, she glanced into his trash can. A piece of gum sat atop a used tissue.

Either would work.

A fist pounded against the wood, and a deep male voice called out, "Let me in, Prentice."

While the mayor walked to the door, Eve pulled an evidence bag from her purse and reached into the trash, scooping the gum and tissue inside it.

"What does he want?" the mayor asked.

Eve turned to find him staring at her as he asked the question. Had he seen what she'd done? She didn't think so, or he would've probably asked what she was doing. But she couldn't be certain…

Of anyone…

Not even Hoge.

Because maybe the mayor was right. Maybe Hoge's father was the killer.

Chapter Seventeen

Hoge's heart hammered like he hammered his fist against the door to the mayor's office. Why had Prentice locked it?

What kind of private meeting was he having with Eve that he'd wanted to ensure no interruptions?

"Let me in!" he yelled again, but he turned toward Alice as well and repeated the order. Surely the receptionist had a key to the mayor's office.

But she shook her head. "Hoge, I'm sure she's fine."

Obviously she'd picked up on his concern for the consultant. Was Eve okay? Somebody had threatened her—may have even tried to kill her last night. She wasn't safe with anyone—not even the mayor.

Maybe especially not the mayor...

The door rattled as the lock turned, and then it opened to the mayor's flushed face. "What do you think you're doing interrupting a meeting in my office like this?" Prentice imperiously demanded to know. He acted more like a king than a mayor, like he was town royalty or something.

How could he and his brother be so different?

Hoge peered over the mayor's head and into the office. "Eve?" he called out. "Are you all right?"

She moved into his line of vision then, walking closer to the door. But she hesitated an arm's length from the mayor, as if she didn't trust him either. And her hand was inside her bulging bag. On her can of pepper spray?

The panic pressing on his chest eased, and his heart rate slowed. She was safe—probably because she was so suspicious of everyone. She even looked at him now with that suspicion back in her pretty blue eyes.

She wouldn't have kissed him the night before if she'd had doubts about him. What had the mayor done? What had Paul Prentice told her to make her look at him that way again?

Paul was the only one in the office with her. Alice had admitted that the mayor had told her not to interrupt this meeting for any reason.

Why had he wanted so desperately to be alone with her?

"Is everything okay?" he asked again.

"No," the mayor replied. "You've really overstepped this time, Hoge. You're trespassing and barging into a private meet—"

"Why?" Hoge asked. "Why is it private? Why would you want to meet with Ms. Collins alone when we're both working the cold cases?"

"Are you?" the mayor asked. "You haven't seemed particularly interested in them until her arrival in town. And now you seem almost too interested..."

"I could say the same about you," Hoge replied. But were they talking about the cases now or Eve? He couldn't be certain. He was interested in Eve—more than interested—*intrigued*.

Was Paul?

He was married, but gossip claimed that hadn't stopped him in the past. Those rumors of extramarital affairs might have been the reason his political career had never really taken off as he'd wanted.

As he'd tried...

So he kept coming back to Cold Creek. Just like the killer must have when he'd committed those three murders over the course of six years. Could Paul Prentice be the killer?

And Eve had been locked alone in the man's office with him...

Hoge shuddered at the thought of what could've happened to her, at what had happened to those other women. "Eve, we should get back to the police department," he told her, desperate to get her out of there.

The mayor stood between them. Was he blocking Hoge from getting inside or blocking her from leaving?

"He's right," Eve said. "I do need to leave." But again, she didn't move closer to the mayor; instead she waited until he stepped aside before she walked toward the door.

But before she could walk through it, Prentice reached out and grasped her forearm. "You'll do what I said," he told her, as if she had no choice.

Hoge's hand curled into a fist as fury gripped him that the man was touching her. But before he could react, Eve tugged free of the mayor's grasp. Instead of balking at his order though, she nodded in acceptance of whatever secret command the mayor had given her.

"What?" Hoge asked her as she passed through the door and joined him in the reception area. "What does he want you to do?"

"It's none of your business, Hoge," the mayor admonished him.

"Everything that has to do with these cold cases is my business," Hoge said.

Eve's eyes widened as if his comment shocked her.

He reminded her and the mayor, "I'm the sheriff. These are my cases to work."

The mayor smirked. "Yet somehow I think my consultant will be the one solving them, Hoge. So you'd better prepare yourself." After uttering his strange warning, he closed his office door in Hoge's face.

He turned toward Eve now. Even though she stood near him, there was more than a door between them. There were walls. Whatever had happened last night must have meant nothing to her. He must have meant nothing to her...because she stared at him as if he were a stranger.

One she had no intention of confiding in because when he asked, as they walked down the stairs to the lobby, what the mayor had asked her to do, she just shrugged off the question.

"He wants me to solve the cases," she replied.

Hoge scoffed. "He never wanted them solved before. In fact, when I first got elected, he encouraged me to leave the cold cases alone."

"He did?"

"Yeah, he didn't want the bad publicity for the town," he said. But now he wondered...

Was it the town Paul Prentice had worried about or himself? Was the real reason he hadn't encouraged the investigation the fact that he was responsible for the murders? Was he the killer?

If so, he would've hardly ordered Eve to solve them.

Unless he intended to make certain she had no way of revealing what she discovered because he intended to kill her before she could expose him.

"What's wrong?"

Eve tensed at the question, but this time it wasn't coming from Hogan Moore. Her father asked, so she couldn't evade or lie to him like she had the sheriff. In fact she was actually relieved to answer him—because it would explain why she was leaving.

She'd asked him to meet her at the café for lunch, so that she could tell him she was going out of town. But she hadn't touched her bowl of cheesy potato soup despite the scent of the chunks of bacon and chives wafting from it. That was probably how her father had figured out something was wrong: she wasn't hungry.

Her father leaned across the table, pitched his voice lower and asked, "Are you going to tell me what it is?"

"I'm leaving town," she admitted.

His brow furrowed. "What? You're not done here. You don't know who the killer is."

"I might have enough to find out," she said, and she ran a hand over the bag she clutched at her side of the booth. "I have to travel a couple of hours to a lab and run some DNA tests."

Her father's shoulders sagged slightly as tension drained from him. "Oh, so you'll be back."

"I can't tell if you're relieved that I might have a lead or that I'm not leaving Cold Creek," she said. "Do you actually like it here?"

He chuckled slightly. "I do. There's something about the small town and the nature that makes me feel more at peace than I've been in a long time."

"Hoge calls it God's country," she murmured. And he'd looked so at peace standing on the deck of that rustic cabin.

"It is God's country," her father agreed. "So peaceful and beautiful…"

Maybe he liked it so much because he'd spent so many years locked in prison, away from nature. Maybe that was why he hadn't been as at peace as he was now—because he still hadn't had his reputation cleared. She needed to make sure that happened. Soon…

"You'll be at peace if this DNA pans out," she said. "I might have discovered who the killer is."

He narrowed his warm blue eyes and studied her face. "Why don't you sound happy about it then? It's all you've wanted for years."

"It should be all you've wanted too," she said with a surge of her old frustration with him. "You should want to know who did what he did to you."

And if it was Hoge's father, what would it mean for her and Hoge? They could never be together. But even if Hoge's father wasn't the killer, they couldn't have ever been together. Unlike her father, there was nothing for her in Cold Creek. Being here had brought her anything but peace.

Her father smiled. "I let go of my anger long ago, Evie. Even without knowing who it was, I forgave him."

She shook her head. "I don't know how. He hasn't paid for what he's done…to anyone. There wasn't just you and those women. He locked a toddler in a trunk during one of the murders here. He's just…" Her voice cracked as emotion overwhelmed her. That poor child had probably grown up with the same phobia Hoge had. How couldn't he have—after the trauma he must have endured?

"That's terrible," her father said. "I am glad you have a lead. But why aren't you happier about it?"

She sighed. "For one, because the man's already dead…"

"He isn't able to hurt anyone else then," her father pointed out, as always finding the positive in a negative situation. Just as he had in prison…

"But he will," she whispered. "He'll hurt Hoge. The mayor thinks Hoge's father was the killer."

"Oh…" Her father leaned back against the booth, sadness pulling at his mouth. "That will hurt Hoge."

"Unless he already knows…" she murmured. Then that would hurt her—because it would mean that he was probably the one who'd written that note warning her away from investigating the case. She shuddered at the thought that she might have kissed the man who'd threatened her.

But he hadn't locked them in the vault. Someone else had done that, or had it all just been an accident or a joke like the mayor had tried to convince her?

Her father sighed wearily before reaching across the table for her hand. He squeezed it gently even as he shook his head, as if he was disappointed in her.

"What's wrong?" she parroted the question he'd asked her.

"You, Evie. You're wrong…with all your doubts about the sheriff. He's a good man."

"You only have Hoge's word that his father was a good man," she said. "He could have been blinded by him…" Like her mother's lies had blinded her. The ten years that her father had been in prison Eve had thought he'd abandoned them—that was the lie her mother had told them. That he'd left. That he didn't care about them...

Pain gripped her heart like it had then—when her mother had told her those terrible lies. Not to protect her. But to protect her own reputation; she hadn't wanted to be known as the wife of a killer, so she'd forced them to move away and change their names. It wasn't until someone from the Innocence Project had contacted her that Eve had learned the truth, that her father was in prison for a crime he hadn't committed. But he'd been more upset about not being able to contact his daughter than he'd been about serving time for another man's crime. She'd been furious about all the years they'd lost that they could have been in contact.

"I'm talking about Hoge," he said. "He's a good man. He wouldn't hide a killer—for any reason. And he wouldn't threaten you."

She gasped that he'd picked up on doubts she hadn't even uttered. But her father was a perceptive man—so perceptive that perhaps he was right about Hogan Moore. Maybe Hoge really was a good man. That was what she'd seen in him, in his interactions with others and with her. Even as scared as he'd been in the vault, he'd comforted her.

"You need to let yourself trust people again, Evie," he said. "You need to open your heart."

She shook her head. "If I do, I'll only get hurt again," she said with certainty.

"Maybe," he acknowledged. "But if that happens,

you'll move on. The only way you'll find true happiness is if you risk getting hurt."

"I'd rather get hurt working a case than falling in love," she admitted.

"I don't want you getting hurt either way," her father said. "So let me go with you…when you go to this lab."

She shook her head. "I don't know how long it might take. You'd be bored."

He shrugged. "I'll find ways to occupy myself."

But she would be distracted, and with the two DNA samples to run she couldn't afford to be distracted right now. "I'll be fine, Dad," she assured him. "I'll probably be safer because I won't be in Cold Creek. I won't be gone long. A university just a couple of hours away has a DNA machine that I can use."

The professor in charge of the university lab had been thrilled to help her out on solving a cold case. Like Hoge, he was aware of her reputation.

"Are you sure you want to do this?" her father asked. "I'm assuming that Hoge doesn't know you're running his father's DNA. How did you even get a sample?"

"I'm not running Rolland Moore's DNA," she said lowly. "I'm running his son's."

"Without his knowledge?" her father asked.

Heat rushed to her face, and she nodded. It wasn't like she'd rummaged through his trash or anything. Although she would have at the Jameses' house had he not stopped her. She was so desperate to find this killer that she wasn't even sure she recognized herself anymore. But it had been too long; she needed to clear her father's name. She needed justice. Now.

She sighed. "I have to, Dad."

Because if she told Hoge what she was doing, she'd

be tipping him off—if he was the one who'd threatened her. She didn't want to believe that he was, though.

"I think you're wasting your time," her father said.

"I have another sample I'm going to test," she admitted.

"From whom?" he asked.

"The mayor," she said in hushed tones. "And no, he isn't aware that I got his DNA either."

"So none of this will be admissible if you actually find the killer," her father said.

"If it matches, I'll work on getting another sample— with a warrant," she explained. But she didn't have the time or the patience to wait for warrants right now and no amount of prayers would help her. Only finding out the truth once and for all...

She'd never used these methods before. She'd always followed the order of the law. But this was different. This was personal—not just because of her father—but because she'd been threatened, she'd been locked in that vault. She was going to protect herself.

From the killer and from falling for the wrong man again.

"I also want to collect some more samples to run," she admitted, "but I need your help."

He narrowed his eyes. "What? How?"

"I need to collect DNA from some of the other guests at the B and B," she said. And she hoped one of them would match the killer or at least be a familial link because she didn't want Hoge to be. "And I need help breaking into their rooms."

"Okay," her father replied.

"Really?" she asked, surprised that he hadn't protested.

"I know you're going to do it anyway," he said. "At least, with my help, hopefully you won't get caught. Because if one of them is the killer..."

She would be in even more danger than she already was.

Chapter Eighteen

After interrupting her strange secret meeting with the mayor, Hoge had requested that Eve share a file with him. He'd wanted to know about the other murder she had definitively linked, with DNA, to the Cold Creek killer. Although she'd kept insisting there were no clues in it to lead to the killer, Eve had returned to the sheriff's office with him and printed off all the information she'd accessed.

Hoge suspected she wouldn't have had to, though, that she was so familiar with that case that she could have recited every bit of evidence and every police interview without showing him anything. Another man had been convicted of the crime—had served ten years on scant circumstantial evidence. The victim and suspect had worked together at the same insurance brokerage, where the victim was a receptionist. A witness, who didn't testify at the trial, claimed to have seen them together the night the victim was found murdered.

The suspect claimed he was just working late but hadn't had an alibi. At the time of the trial, the forensic experts had claimed they hadn't found any DNA on the victim.

But nearly a decade later, a justice league had rerun the evidence and found plenty, and none of it had matched the suspect who'd already served so many years for a crime he hadn't committed.

The killer had locked Peter B. Delaney in prison as effectively as he'd locked Loretta James's little boy in that trunk. And Tom Wilson...

That was the name of the witness who'd disappeared, who'd never been found, who the prosecutor had claimed Peter B. Delaney must have killed before trial so the judge had allowed Tom's statement to the police into evidence. Tom had to be the killer...

But who was Tom Wilson? Really...

Because Hoge doubted that was even his name. He was also surprised that there was so much information in this file that Eve had downplayed. There was more here than in the files in the vault.

Hoge had questions for her—so many questions—but after printing everything, she'd left to meet her father for lunch. And she had yet to return.

Hoge had been so interested in the file, and in looking for something else, that he hadn't noticed until now how long she'd been gone. Like he and Eve had researched the other victims, he'd researched Samantha Otten, the young receptionist who'd been attending night school. On her memorial social media page, which her younger sister had set up, he'd found the necklace.

The very same necklace...

The killer must have romanced and gifted every victim with this same necklace before killing them. Hoge had spent so much time studying the pendant, looking for that specific nick in it, that he hadn't really focused on the chain—until he noticed on the victim's social media page how strong it looked, like it could have been used as the weapon that had strangled the victims.

The realization brought on a wave of horror and sympathy but also determination. As Eve had said, they were getting close. Eager to share his discovery with her, he rushed over to the B and B. But once again, he found that the only Collins inside the big Queen Anne was her father. He was in the lounge engaged in a game of chess with Bob Dempski.

"Hi there, Hoge," the former deputy greeted him. "I've found an opponent as savvy as your father. If only Rolland were still alive to play him…"

With a grin, Mr. Collins took his opponent's king and exclaimed, "Checkmate."

Bob chuckled and stood up from the table. "Your turn, Hoge. Maybe you'll have better luck."

"I don't want to interrupt," Hoge said. "You might want a rematch."

"Later," Bob said. "I need to go buy a new toothbrush. I can't find mine. Pam claims she didn't throw it out when she cleaned up, but…" He shrugged. "Who knows…"

Hoge knew. But he waited until the security guard left the lounge before he asked. "Where is she?"

He already knew she was gone because her car hadn't been in the parking lot. But where would she have found a DNA lab? He'd had to send out his evidence to the state police one, but he knew Eve wouldn't trust anyone else to process the DNA she'd collected.

She didn't trust anyone but her father.

Bruce Collins's face was flushed with guilt. He must

have known her plan—or helped her collect that DNA. Hoge suspected the security guard wasn't the only one who would find his toothbrush—or other items— missing.

After getting locked in the vault the night before, he could hardly blame her for wanting to discover who might be threatening her. But if the killer had caught her stealing his DNA…

Or even just suspected, because of a missing tooth-brush, that she'd stolen it…

Her father said nothing as he stared down at the chess board.

"Mr. Collins," Hoge said. "She could be in danger. If anyone suspects that she took his DNA, he could go after her." Like someone had gone after them the night before…

The older man gasped. "I didn't think of that. I was just trying to help her not get caught while she was taking things. But…"

He'd realized what Hoge had—that she didn't necessarily have to be caught in the act to be suspected. Especially when the killer already felt threatened enough to try to get rid of her…

"She could be in serious danger," Hoge pointed out. "Do you know where she is?"

He nodded. "Yes. She refused to let me go with her. She's using a DNA machine at a university lab. It's just a couple of hours from here." The man peered over Hoge's shoulder at the grandfather clock in a corner of the lounge. "I thought she'd be back by now. She left shortly after lunch."

Hoge glanced at his watch. He'd been so caught up in going through the case file that he'd lost track of time. It was even later than he'd thought. As usual he'd forgotten to eat, but the hollow ache inside him didn't feel like hunger.

It felt like fear.

"Call her," he urged her father.

The man nodded. "Yes, of course." He pulled out his cell and punched in the contact for Evie.

"Hello, Dad," she said.

When her voice answered, filled with warmth, the hollowness in Hoge filled with that warmth. She affected him in a way no one else ever had.

"Evie, are you all right?" Mr. Collins asked.

"Yes, of course," she said. "But the equipment here isn't like in my lab. They don't have the rapid DNA testing capabilities I have. I'm going to have to spend the night to await the results."

And the hollowness yawned inside Hoge again. It had nothing to do with having to wait for results though, and everything to do with her being gone for the night.

He wasn't just worried about her safety, though. He was worried about her leaving—for good. Would she even return when she got the results?

"None of her results will be admissible in court," Hoge murmured.

"Who's that?" Eve asked, her voice sharp with alarm as it emanated from her father's phone.

"The sheriff is here with me," Bruce Collins replied. "He's worried about your safety. He was wondering where you've gone."

"You told him?" she asked, and now the sharpness in her voice was betrayal. "Dad…"

"Evie—"

Hoge held out his hand for her father's cell. "May I speak with her?"

Mr. Collins passed over the phone.

"Eve," Hoge began. "You've put yourself in danger."

She made a strange sound, like a gasp. "Are you threatening me?"

"No, I'm not the one threatening you, but apparently you're so intent on figuring out who is that you've broken into rooms and stolen personal items."

"Somebody reported me?" she asked.

"No," he admitted. "I hope nobody realizes you're behind the mysteriously missing things, but if they do…"

"I'm staying right here in the lab," she said. "The university, especially the lab, has high security, so nobody can break in and get to me. I'll be perfectly safe."

His tension eased slightly, but he wasn't entirely assured. "You're going to stay awake all night working and then drive back? Let me meet you there. I'll pick you up."

"You can't drive my car and your SUV both," she said. "I'm fine. Nobody followed me here. And I can sleep on one of the couches in the lab. *I'm* perfectly safe."

Was she implying that someone else wasn't? Like him? Or the men whose DNA she'd collected?

"Please tell my dad that," she said. "And also look out for him for me."

Despite all her suspicions, or maybe because of them, she worried about her father. But at least she'd trusted Hoge enough to ask him to watch over the man she loved most. "I'll make sure that nothing happens to him," he assured her. He only wished he could do the same for her—make sure that she stayed safe.

Because he had a feeling that no matter what she claimed, she was still in danger. If the person hadn't figured out yet that she'd obtained his DNA, he might...

And then he might go looking for her at any nearby labs with a DNA machine. After talking with her, Hoge intended to call a state trooper and make sure she had protection at the campus and on her way back to Cold Creek.

"Just please, make sure that nothing happens to you," he said.

"I will. Goodbye, Hoge..." her voice rasped through the phone, as if she was overwhelmed with emotion.

Was she feeling everything that he was?

That hollowness?

That longing?

He hadn't known her very long but already he missed her. What would he do when she solved the cases and left Cold Creek? Because they were close...

Very close to finding the killer.

He just hoped they found him before the killer found them.

She missed him.

Not her father...

She missed Hoge. She hadn't even missed her ex-fiancé like this. But then she'd been too angry when she discovered he'd been sleeping with her best friend, her college roommate. She'd been so infuriated with them both that she hadn't had time to miss David. But she wondered if she ever would have...

Eve should be furious now, too, but she didn't know
for certain if Hoge knew…that his father was the killer.

Knowing she wouldn't have been able to sleep, she'd
stayed up the entire night running tests on the DNA
she'd extracted from everything she'd collected. Now
she had the results of all of them in her bag, which lay
on the seat next to her as she drove back to Cold Creek.

Hoge's samples were the only ones she'd taken the
time to compare to the killer's DNA profile.

And her stomach had flipped while her heart had
pounded as she'd identified the familial connection.
Father…

Hoge's father was the killer.

He was dead. So there would be no trial; she would
never get the public vindication for her father that he
deserved. Nor the retribution for Hoge's father that *he*
deserved…

He'd escaped that through death, and he'd died his
son's hero. He'd died the town's hero.

Was that why everyone had been so unwelcoming
to her? Had they known that Rolland Moore was the
murderer of those young women so long ago?

Had they wanted to protect his image as much as
his son did? Maybe it wasn't Hoge who'd shoved that
note under her door. There was no way—even if he
could have done it without her noticing—that he would
have closed that vault door on them. Someone else had
done that.

Who?

Who else might want to protect Rolland Moore's
memory? Doreen? The older woman would have been
about his age and must have worked for him for a long
time. And she hadn't wanted to check the vault until

Eve's father had insisted that they should. So maybe Doreen had closed that door and left the note.

Even though the killer was dead, there was still a threat out there. A threat to Eve and maybe even to her father. She needed to get back to Cold Creek. She needed to make sure her dad was all right. And she needed to tell Hoge what she'd learned.

Would he be devastated? Or would he devastate her when he revealed that he'd always known?

She eased her foot slightly off the accelerator, slowing down as dread filled her. She wasn't nearly as anxious now to return—to face Hoge and admit what she'd done, that she'd taken his DNA.

Clearly he hadn't realized that last night. When he'd taken her father's cell and spoken to her, he'd only mentioned the other DNA. From the other B and B guests...

He hadn't known about his own, had probably even forgotten about that granola bar. There had been enough on it for her to extract for a test. A definitive test.

Poor Hoge...

Poor Dad...

Her empathy extended only to those two men, though—not the man who'd sworn to uphold the law only to break it in the most horrible ways...

Murder.

Those women would have known him—just as she and Hoge had guessed. Maybe he'd even given them that peace necklace...only to take it again once he'd shattered their peace and claimed their lives.

The truth coming out would shatter Hoge's life. His whole world...

Tears stung her eyes, but she blinked them back and focused on the road. But not soon enough.

Something slammed into the back of her car, sending it hurtling forward—toward the shoulder of the road. She grasped the steering wheel and tried to maneuver back onto the pavement, but metal crunched as she was struck again.

She glanced into her rearview mirror but could glimpse only the grille of the front of a big vehicle, the vehicle that was shoving hers from the road and into one of those steep ditches on the side of it.

The hood of her vehicle crumpled as it struck the hard ground. Then she struck the steering wheel just as the air bag began to unfurl from it—too late. Her head hit something hard, pain radiating throughout her skull.

She blinked, but she couldn't clear her vision this time. It wasn't tears blinding her but blackness, as oblivion threatened to claim her.

Someone knew where she'd been and maybe what she'd discovered—someone who'd known when she was probably going to return.

Hoge?

He was the last thought on her mind before everything went completely black.

Chapter Nineteen

"Hoge!"

He jumped at the shout, knocking his knee against his desk. He'd been engrossed in the case file Eve had shared with him until Doreen's anxious-sounding voice drew his attention to the doorway where she stood. She was almost shaking with that anxiety.

"What?" he asked with concern. "What's wrong?"

"A motorist spotted a car in a ditch on the highway just outside town."

Not nearly as concerned now, Hoge raised his shoulders. "And? Isn't there a deputy on duty close by to check on the motorist and make sure everyone's okay?"

"The car has an out-of-state plate."

Dread gripped him as he realized why she was so upset and why she thought he'd be so upset. Just moments ago he'd had a call from the state trooper who'd been supposed to follow Eve from campus but had fallen asleep and not noticed when she'd left. He didn't even have to ask from which state the plate came.

"Pennsylvania," she answered for him anyway. "I'm going to go over to the B and B and get Bruce."

"Bruce?" he asked, not immediately placing the name or what her interest in him would be.

The older woman's face flushed. "Mr. Collins…"

Sometime over the past couple of days, Eve's dad had become Bruce to Doreen…just as the consultant had become Eve to Hoge. No. She had become *everything*.

Eve filled his heart with warmth, with comfort… more so than even nature had done for him. She was beautiful—on the outside and the inside too with her love of justice and her father.

She was such a special person and not just to him.

If she'd been hurt…

Or worse…

He didn't know what he was going to do. Except pray…

He was praying right now, praying that she was all right, even as he jumped up and grabbed the keys for his SUV off his desk. He silently spoke to God. *Please, Heavenly Father, please make sure that she's not hurt. That if she is, she'll be okay. She has to be okay. The world needs her. Her father needs her. I…*

He needed her, but he probably didn't deserve her. He could only throw himself on the mercy of his creator, though. *Please, God…*

Then he spoke to Doreen, "I'm going. I'll let you know if you should bring Mr. Collins out to the crash…"

He couldn't say *accident site*. He didn't believe for a moment that it had been an accident. Just as the vault door getting shut on them hadn't been one.

He'd been such a fool to let her stay at the university—to let her drive herself back. He should have insisted on personally protecting her.

With someone threatening her, he never should have let Eve out of his sight…because now he might never get to see her again.

Eve was fine. And for that she was deeply grateful. The first thing she'd done when she'd opened her eyes again was breathe a sigh of relief and a thank you.

Thank you, God. Thank you for protecting me from harm.

She wasn't hurt, but she was furious. She did have a bump on her head and a dull ache throbbing at her temple. She'd lost consciousness but just for a moment… not so long that whoever had run her off the road had had time to finish her off.

No. She'd had time to arm herself with her canister of pepper spray. But whoever had forced her off the road had driven away with a squeal of tires once she'd crashed. She suspected they hadn't called for help either.

And she hadn't been able to either since her cell phone had died sometime during the night. She'd left her charger in her bedroom at the B and B. So she'd had a dead phone and no way to escape her damaged vehicle on her own.

She'd been trapped inside…armed only with the pepper spray that she'd almost used on the motorist who had stopped to check on her.

"I called the police," he'd assured her as if he'd noticed her gripping that can.

Sirens had wailed seconds later. An officer must have been close.

How close?

Close enough to have forced her from the road? It wasn't Hoge who rushed to her vehicle though but the deputy who'd opened the basement door for her a couple of nights ago.

"Ms. Collins, are you all right?" he asked with what seemed like sincere concern.

But Eve didn't trust him. She couldn't trust anyone. "I feel fine," she said. But for the fury...

That continued to course through her, making her pulse pound fast and hard. She tried to pull out the gratitude again—to God and to the deputy—but the anger consumed her now. "I just need to get out of here."

"An engine is coming from the firehouse," he said. "They have the jaws of life. They'll get you out."

"Just break the window," Eve said. Actually the glass of the windshield had already shattered, but it had stayed intact like some bizarre spiderweb.

The deputy shook his head. "You might get cut."

"I'll cover my face," she said. If he didn't break it, she was going to do it herself. She didn't like the feeling of being trapped—not again—not so soon after she'd been shut in that vault.

Her mind flitted to that poor little boy—the one who'd been locked in the trunk of Amy Simpson's car. How long had he been in there? What had he seen and heard before he'd been shut inside?

And how could a lawman, like Sheriff Rolland Moore, have done that to a child?

He'd been a monster—not the man his son believed him to be. Unless his son was also a monster...

But she hadn't seen that in Hoge. She hadn't seen anything but empathy and sincerity and spirituality and goodness.

And now concern…as he jumped into the ditch and rushed up to the passenger's side of her car. "Eve!" he called out, his voice cracking with fear. "Are you all right?"

"Yes," she said, her patience fraying as her fury kept hold of her. "I just want out. Now!"

He—more than anyone—understood her need to escape. "Cover your face," he told her. And once she had, she heard a sharp explosion then the tinkling of glass.

Had he shot out the window?

It wasn't a gun he slid back onto his police belt, though, but a thin metal baton. Then he knocked out the rest of the glass of the passenger's window and, leaning through it, reached across the seat for her.

She hesitated for a long moment, the fury turning to fear as it pounded in her veins and in her heart.

"Are you okay?" he asked. "Can't you move?"

"I don't have any injuries," she insisted. She'd struck her head, but she'd only lost consciousness for a moment or two. She was fine, but her hand trembled when she unclasped her seat belt. Then she crawled across the console. His hands on her arms, he helped her through the window and then into his embrace.

He clutched her closely, against his madly pounding heart, for a long moment. "Are you all right?"

She wasn't…because she should be pulling away from him. Maybe she'd been hurt, or was in shock, and that was why she couldn't move away. Why she leaned against him…

Why her arms closed around his back for a moment and she clung to him. That was only to keep herself upright…

Not because his warmth comforted her…

Not because she needed him.

She couldn't need someone she couldn't trust. What if he was the one...?

She shuddered and pulled back from him, but her foot slipped in the mud at the bottom of the ditch. And she stumbled back against the side of her crumpled car.

"I'm sorry," he said. "You're standing in water. Let's get you out of here." His arm around her, he helped her up the bank of the steep ditch to the street.

The fire engine had arrived; it was parked behind Hoge's SUV. But he held up a hand to them. "She's out. I'll take her to the ER to get checked out," he told them, knowing that would be faster than waiting for an ambulance. "We'll only need a wrecker to pull out her car now." He turned away from the firemen and his deputy.

"What happened?" he asked her, but he was staring at the rear bumper of her vehicle and she knew he knew.

But was that the only reason why? Because it was obvious what had happened...or because he'd done it?

She didn't want to think that—didn't want to think that he could have tried to hurt her. But she knew how much he loved his dad, how much he cherished memories of the man. "Someone forced me off the road," she replied. "Someone tried to kill me."

"Eve—" He reached for her again, but she flinched and shrank back.

Hurt crossed his face and then alarm. "You don't seriously think that I would hurt you. You can't..."

That hurt touched her heart, squeezing it tightly. She didn't want to suspect him of anything but being the good, sincere man she'd started to think he was. That was the man she'd kissed, the one she'd begun to fall for...

But what if his love for his father was more important to him than whatever he might have begun to feel for her?

"I know that you would do anything to protect the image you have of your father," she said, her heart aching with her pain and his.

His brow furrowed. "What are you talking about? What does my father have to do with your getting run off the road? He's been dead two years."

"And maybe you thought it was over then, that nobody would ever find out," she murmured. "But I found out. I know the truth."

"What are you talking about?" he asked. And he reached out again, toward her forehead.

But she jerked back again.

"You have a bump on your head," he said. "You must be disoriented, confused…"

She shook her head, and though pain reverberated inside it, her mind was clear. "I have proof," she said.

As he'd warned last night, though, it wouldn't be admissible in court. But then a prosecutor couldn't bring charges against a dead man anyway.

But the live one, the one who'd tried to kill her…

Could it have been Hoge? She didn't want to believe it. Just as he probably didn't want to believe what she was saying.

"Eve, I don't understand what you're talking about…" he murmured.

"I know who the killer is," she said. "*Your father* was the killer."

All the color drained from his face then, but that was his only reaction. She watched for it—for any flicker of it—but there wasn't.

He wasn't surprised at all.

"You knew," she said, and that fury coursed through her again like a fire through dead brush. Hot and fast and full of destruction. It destroyed all the trust she had begun to have for him, all the feelings…

Or at least she hoped it did—because she couldn't care about someone who'd protected a murderer. Especially one who might have gone to such great lengths to protect that murderer that he'd threatened and nearly killed her.

Others had betrayed her.

Had hurt her…

Her mother with her lies about her father, claiming that he'd abandoned them. That he'd left them…and that was why they had to leave town, why they'd had to change their names. She'd only been ten then, so she hadn't asked the questions she should have.

Ten years later, she'd been lied to again. Her ex-fiancé and her friend had made fools of her, sneaking around behind her back like she would never find out about them. Like she would never know that while David had professed his love for her, his willingness to wait for their marriage…he'd been sleeping with another woman, a woman who'd claimed to be her best friend.

But none of that hurt like this did, like Hogan Moore's betrayal hurt her. She had really started falling for him—maybe she already had.

Chapter Twenty

"You knew he was the killer!" Eve said.

Some part of him had always known, had always at least suspected, that his father might be the killer. But how could she know...

When he didn't even...

"How?" he asked. "How did you find this out?"

She turned toward him from where she sat in the passenger seat of his SUV. He was surprised she'd gotten inside with him to ride back to Cold Creek—after the way she'd reacted to him at the crash site, like she either blamed him for forcing her off the road or feared him.

Just because of what his father was...

A killer.

"I got your DNA off the granola bar you ate in the vault," she admitted. "I ran it against the DNA from the old crime scenes and concluded there was a familial match. Father and son..."

He gasped for breath, feeling as if he'd been sucker punched. So he pulled the SUV onto the shoulder of the road and stopped it before he wound up in the ditch like she had.

"Don't act surprised now," she said. "When I first told you, I could tell that you already knew. How could you…" She shook her head as if disgusted. "How could you idolize a man who murdered so many women?"

"Idolize? What are you talking about?" he asked. "I didn't even know him. I still don't know him."

"The sheriff—"

"Rolland Moore is—*was*—my adoptive father," he explained. "He was not my biological dad. Rolland found me at the scene of Amy Simpson's murder."

She gasped now, her blue eyes wide with shock behind the lenses of her glasses. "Oh, Hoge, you were the baby…"

"And Rolland Moore is the one who rescued me from the trunk. And when my family refused to take me back after my babysitter died, like I was somehow responsible for the murders, he talked his wife into adopting me and acting like I was theirs."

"You made it sound like she died," she said.

"My real mother," he said. "Loretta James died. Rolland's wife had already left him. She'd grown tired of Cold Creek long before I came along. For a bigger divorce settlement, she agreed to adopt me with the sheriff. She kept me outside town for a while, so that she could bring me back as a surprise she had after leaving him. Then she made a big show of dumping me on him to raise on his own, making everybody believe that I was his biological child."

"Why all the subterfuge?" she asked.

"To protect me," Hoge explained. "To protect me from the stigma of being *that* baby…" His voice cracked as he remembered all the things that had been said about Loretta James's son. "That bad luck or attractor of evil that my biological family thought I was." That was why he'd never risked a relationship, because he'd worried that they might be right about that, that he might put anyone close to him in danger. And he had...

Rolland had died.

Eve had been run off the road.

Tears streamed down her face now. "So Rolland Moore really was the man you remember him being."

Tears stung Hoge's eyes, but he blinked them back and steered the SUV back onto the road, toward the town his father had served and protected as best he could. "He was a hero," he said. "My hero."

"He was like my dad then," Eve said. "He was a good man."

"Yes," Hoge said. "That's why it haunted him that he was never able to find the killer. Not just for those women but for me, as well."

"Hoge..."

She reached across the console, but he was the one who jerked away now, not wanting her to touch him.

"Did you purposely shut us in that vault?" he asked. "Was that some kind of ploy to get my DNA? The granola bar? The *kiss*?" His heart pounded with the suspicions suddenly assailing him. If that hadn't been real...

She gasped again. "How could you think that?"

"You were between me and the door. I was distracted with those photo albums. You could have pulled it shut without me noticing..." He shuddered. "Until it was too late..."

"I wouldn't have done that."

"And the kiss?" he asked, his heart aching with the pain that it hadn't been real. That she'd only played him in order to solve the cold cases. "You don't trust me, let alone like me. I should have known it was all some kind of setup, just like stealing things from the rooms of the other guests at the B and B. All that matters to you is finding this killer. Why? Do you and the mayor have another press conference planned?"

"You don't trust me either," she said. "You haven't trusted me since I came to town."

"Because I know you have another interest in these cases, some kind of personal stake…"

"Like you," she said. "You've been investigating your mother's murder. You were a witness."

He snorted. "A witness who doesn't remember anything…" But the dark…but the screams…

"And still you were a more reliable witness than the one in the last murder investigation," she murmured.

"What is it, Eve?" he asked, but he wasn't really expecting her to answer him.

"My father," she said.

"What? Your dad isn't the killer." He knew just as he knew Rolland Moore wasn't.

She shook her head, and a tress of blond hair brushed against his shoulder. "No, he isn't, and I'm glad you realize that. Other law enforcement officers weren't as astute as you are. He did ten years in prison for one of the murders…"

"Peter B. Delaney," he said. "That's his real name." There had been a picture in the file, but the man had seemed so much larger than her father, heavier, younger. But that had happened nearly two decades ago, and prison had clearly affected him physically.

But not spiritually…

Bruce Collins was a good man.

"Yeah, you're not the only one whose name was

changed to escape a stigma," she murmured. "First my mother changed it—when she claimed my father deserted us, but she was the one who made us move away from town. It was only later that I learned the truth, that he'd been arrested and convicted for a crime he hadn't committed. The justice league that was working to free him contacted me when I was in college."

"He got out," Hoge said.

She nodded. "Just like you got out of that trunk all those years ago."

"I had help," he said. "I couldn't have done it on my own."

"Neither could he," she said. "A lot of people worked together to free him."

"Your mother?"

She scoffed. "Not her. She's still convinced he's guilty. I think she clings to that to excuse what she did, how she lied to me."

Now Hoge understood why Eve struggled to trust anyone but her father.

"I'm sorry," he said. He was so very sorry…

Because now he knew for certain that they would never have a future, that she would never be able to forgive the pain and suffering his father had caused her. She already hadn't trusted him; now she never would.

"You could have just asked," he said.

"What?"

"For my DNA," he said. "You could have just asked. You didn't have to trick me."

"I—I didn't lock us in the vault," she said. "And I didn't…"

"Kiss me for it?" he asked.

She shook her head. "No."

He wanted to ask her why she'd kissed him then, but it didn't matter now. She already hadn't trusted him, and now she never would because of who—and *what*—his father was.

A murderer...

A monster...

Hoge had always suspected, but now that he knew for certain he felt sick. That was another reason why he had vowed to stay single because of his fear he was related to the killer. That he carried the same genetics as a monster, a murderer...

He would forever be haunted that he might be capable of that kind of violence himself. So it would be best for him and for whatever woman he fell for to remain single forever.

Eve was in shock. Not from the crash, which she now rested from in her room at the B and B, but from all Hogan Moore had revealed to her. Moore wasn't his real last name. James was. At least, it had been his mother's last name. What was his father's?

Who was his father...besides a killer?

She remembered how she'd felt when she'd finally learned that her father was in prison, how sick at heart she'd been suspecting, for just a short while, that he might have been a murderer...

She shuddered at those horrific memories.

"Are you okay?" her father asked. He'd not left her room since the sheriff had dropped her back at the Queen Anne after taking her to the ER.

Her father had already known what had happened when they'd found him in the lounge with Doreen, who'd been holding his hand. When had her father gotten close to the dispatcher?

The dispatcher whom Eve had considered might have shut her and Hoge in the vault.

Hoge thought she'd done that...

Hurt and irritation burned her heart. She didn't like being suspected of such subterfuge. And she felt a flash of guilt for all she'd presumed about him. Of hiding his father's guilt...

Of trying to run her off the road.

She'd imagined far worse of him than he had of her. And she had done far worse than he had. She had taken Pam's keys from the hook in the kitchen and let herself into the other guests' rooms. She'd stolen things from them.

And even before that, she hadn't been entirely honest with Hoge. He had every reason to mistrust her.

That bothered her so much that she felt some strange hollow ache inside her. Maybe she was just hungry. Maybe she shouldn't have rejected Doreen's offer to bring her dinner.

Eve had said that she'd just wanted to be alone for a while, to rest, since she hadn't slept at all the night before. But her father must have sensed she needed him—or he was afraid to leave her alone—because he'd come up to her room shortly after her.

"Eve, what's wrong?" her father asked.

"Everything..." she murmured and nearly smiled at how dramatic she sounded, like a teenager. Her father had missed her teenage years; he'd been in prison from the time she was ten to when she'd turned twenty.

"I thought the ER said you were fine. Should we go

back or find a better doctor?" he asked. "I'm sure Doreen will know—"

"I'm sure she will," she said. She'd suspected, from the way she'd talked about him, that Doreen must have had a crush on Rolland Moore. Now, knowing what the man had done for Hoge—how he'd rescued and safeguarded him—she understood why. Rolland Moore sounded protective, self-sacrificing, loving...

Like Hoge...

Tears stung her eyes, but she blinked them back. "I screwed up, Daddy," she admitted.

"Oh, Evie..." He sat on the bed next to her and pulled her into his comforting embrace.

"I screwed up with Hoge. He hates me."

Her father chuckled. "I doubt that. I think he cares about you very much."

Maybe he had; maybe he'd begun to have the feelings for her that she had for him. But not now...

"He wasn't happy that I took his DNA."

"The DNA..." her father murmured, and he pulled back to study her face. "What did you learn?"

"The mayor was right. Hoge's father is the killer," she said.

Her father gasped and shook his head. "I wouldn't have believed it after everything I've heard about Rolland—"

"Rolland Moore isn't his biological father," she said. "The former sheriff adopted Hoge...after finding him in the trunk of the car of the second murder victim. Hoge was the son of the first..."

Her father inhaled sharply. "And his biological father murdered both women?"

She nodded.

"Poor Hoge…" His voice was gruff with the pain he must've felt for the younger man. "Did he know?"

She shrugged. "I think he suspected, but he didn't know for certain…until I accused him of idolizing a killer. I didn't know he'd been adopted. I didn't know who he really was…"

"A good man," her father said. "He's a good man. He'll understand. You need to tell him everything, Eve."

"I did," she admitted. "And he apologized, like it was somehow his fault…" Like he was taking responsibility for the sins of his biological father.

Her father shook his head. "He's not to blame for any of this. You know that now, right? That he wasn't the one who threatened you?"

Tears rushed up on her again, as she thought of the accusations that she'd hurled at him. "I knew how much he idolized Rolland Moore. So I thought he might do anything to protect the man's memory…"

"Even threaten you?" her father asked.

"I know what I would do to protect you," she said.

"You wouldn't hurt anyone else. Or at least I didn't think you would. But you hurt Hoge, suspecting the worst of him," her father said, and now there was disappointment in his voice. "I know that what you've been through with me, your mother, your former fiancé… has affected your ability to trust, Evie. But there are good, honest people in this world. More good than bad. You need to believe that. You need to find your faith in people again."

"You're right," she conceded. "I know you're right."

"You can trust the sheriff," he said. "He wouldn't have threatened you. I would hope you'd have faith in him, in yourself and in the feelings you obviously have for him. I wish you would trust your heart as much as you trust science, Evie."

She'd run more than the test on Hoge's DNA, but once she'd found that Hoge's father was the killer, she'd assumed he was dead. And she hadn't looked at the other results. But his biological father could still be alive…

Was probably still alive…and threatening her.

Who was he? Did she already know?

Did she already have his DNA?

Chapter Twenty-One

Hoge shouldn't have dropped her off at the B and B like he had. He shouldn't have let her out of his sight again. Not when someone had just tried to kill her...

But he trusted her father to keep her safe. And he doubted the man would let her out of his sight now. Doreen had confirmed as much when she'd exited the Queen Anne and found him sitting in his SUV outside it.

"Are you okay?" she'd asked him.

He wasn't, but he'd forced himself to nod at the dispatcher and assure her that he was. He needed to be... for Eve. Someone had tried to kill her and would probably try again.

His father?

Was that who'd locked them in the vault? Who'd run her off the road?

She'd stolen DNA from everyone staying at the B and B. Had she checked all of them against the killer or just his?

Hoge needed to know. Or maybe he already did...

His father was the killer. He'd eluded justice for all

these years, so he was smart. He'd killed in one other state that they knew of, so he traveled.

That eliminated Lenny, the café cook, and Bob, the security guard. Even after retiring from the police department, Bob had refused to travel with his wife—which might have led to their separation and his stay at the B and B.

So…

His stomach lurched, as a suspicion crept into his mind…making his heart pound fast and hard. He remembered the files Eve had printed off for him. The name of the place her father had worked, where the secretary had been murdered, and he'd been accused of that murder solely on circumstantial evidence.

He knew.

His hand shaking, he reached for his cell. It began to vibrate in his pocket before he extracted it, startling him. He grabbed for it and recognized the number. Eve…

She couldn't know what he knew, though. She wouldn't have the DNA of the man he suspected, not from anything she'd taken at the B and B.

Before he could answer, the call ended. He breathed a sigh of relief that was short-lived when fingers tapped the glass of the passenger window. He glanced up to find her standing outside his SUV.

He pressed the unlock button, and she pulled open the passenger door.

"Were you ignoring my call?" she asked.

He shook his head. "Didn't have time to answer…"

"I saw you…" She turned toward him, her gaze intent on his face. "Have you been here since you dropped me off?"

He nodded.

"You didn't have to stay," she said. "My father was by my side the entire time." She pointed out the window to where Mr. Collins stood on the porch, waving at Hoge.

Looking at the man caused Hoge's heart to ache as he thought of the years Peter Bruce Delaney had lost because of *his* father. The man, who called himself Bruce now, turned and walked back into the B and B.

"He trusts you with me?" Hoge murmured, wondering why...

"Yes," Eve said. "He told me to call you. That you deserve to know..."

He suspected he already did. "You know who the killer is?"

She nodded. "I do."

"But how? The guests' DNA..."

"Wasn't the only DNA I processed."

He still wasn't sure that she knew what he'd put together. He wasn't even sure that he was right. But Hoge started the SUV and pulled onto the street.

Eve grasped the armrest and then reached for her seat belt. "You know?" she asked with surprise.

"It just occurred to me," he admitted. "That's why I was sitting here." He was stunned, as in shock as she'd probably been from her crash. If he was right...

Then his world was nearly as shattered as it would have been had the killer actually been Rolland Moore.

He didn't drive far, just to city hall. The mayor wasn't waiting for them in his office; he was already in the parking lot, climbing into his SUV. He stopped, with the driver's door open, when Hoge parked next to him.

Prentice ignored him and focused on Eve. "Ms. Collins, I've been expecting an update from you regarding what we spoke about last time." He cast a furtive glance at Hoge.

"You told her to run my DNA," he said. She hadn't set him up in the vault as a ploy to collect it herself. She'd just been sweet and comforting to him because that was her nature, no matter how hard she tried to hide it—to protect herself from more of the pain untrustworthy people had caused her.

He understood that now. He'd trusted someone he shouldn't have, as well.

The mayor's face flushed. "Yes, I did. It never made sense to me that your father couldn't solve those murders."

"That was because he knew the killer," Hoge said.

Paul snorted. "Of course he did. Your father wasn't the saint this town has painted him to be—"

"Rolland Moore wasn't the killer!" Eve interjected. "He was the saint this town believes he was."

And Hoge's heart warmed with her defense of his father, of his real father—the man who'd loved and protected him, just as he'd loved and tried to protect Cold Creek.

"If he wasn't the killer, why couldn't he find the killer?" The mayor scoffed. "Was he protecting him?"

"No, he never suspected the man," Hoge said. And neither had he...

No matter how close their friendship, Rolland Moore wouldn't have covered for him. Hoge wasn't so sure about the mayor, though. He might have known and hidden the truth in order to protect himself from scandal.

"What is he talking about?" Paul asked Eve. "He's not making any sense. You only took his DNA."

She shook her head. "I took yours, too."

He gasped, and so did Hoge.

Now he knew how she knew. A smile tugged at his lips over how smart she was. Or maybe it was just her suspicious nature that had made her test everyone through anything she could find.

"What—how?" Prentice asked, appalled. "I didn't give you a swab."

"I took some gum from your trash can," she admitted. "I ran it. You and the sheriff are actually related, you know."

Hoge's stomach lurched at the thought. Not of being related to Paul but of being related to a killer.

The mayor sneered. "No, that makes no sense. I am not related to Rolland Moore."

"Neither am I by blood," Hoge admitted. "But I am biologically related to the killer. He is my father."

"And from the DNA profiles, I've determined he's your brother," Eve said.

Paul shook his head. "No. That makes no sense. None of this makes sense…"

"But it does," Hoge said. It suddenly all made sense to him. And Eve had been right when she'd accused him of idolizing a murderer. He had—because he had always idolized the man he'd called Uncle Ted.

Eve had all the DNA evidence to support her discovery, but there was so much she still didn't know. So much that she suspected the sheriff had already figured out.

But he said nothing now, just stood silently beside the door the mayor had closed and locked behind them when he'd insisted on continuing their meeting in his office—probably where nobody would overhear them, as might have been the case in the parking lot. Obviously he didn't want anyone to know that he was related to the killer.

But the truth was going to come out now. No matter how much he might not want it to.

"I can't believe you stole gum out of my trash," the mayor said, staring into the empty can as if somehow wishing it back. "That you suspected me..."

"She suspected everyone," Hoge said, finally speaking again—but *for* her instead of *to* her.

The mayor shook his head. "But none of it makes sense. You must have mixed up the results or something..."

"No, I didn't," she said. "If you want to give me another sample, I'll run it again. But you must know you have a familial relationship to the killer."

The mayor's face, which had flushed earlier, paled now, and he dropped into the chair behind his desk. "I really don't have a relationship with him. You do, Hoge. You and your..." He gasped as realization dawned on him. He must have finally processed what they'd told him in the parking lot. Hoge was his brother's biological son and therefore his nephew.

"Where is he?" Hoge asked. "Do you know where he is?"

Prentice shook his head. "I don't know. He must be traveling for business. He's always traveling..."

And killing. How many victims were there? How many more would there be if he wasn't apprehended soon?

"He's here," Hoge said. "He has to be the one who forced Ms. Collins off the road earlier today."

The mayor gasped again. "When? What happened?"

"He tried to kill her," Hoge said. "Maybe he knew she had the results. Or he just knew that she was going to be the one to figure it out, to prove his guilt."

The mayor shook his head and kept shaking it as he murmured, "No… It's not possible… It can't be Ted."

"Where would he be?" Hoge persisted.

The mayor looked up again, his gaze meeting the sheriff's. "You would know better than I would."

And Hoge sucked in a breath with what must have been his realization.

"Where?" Eve asked. The man hadn't checked back into the B and B, probably because he hadn't wanted Eve to have access to any of his DNA.

Hoge didn't answer her. He reached for the door, unlocked and pulled it open.

Before he could walk out, Eve jumped up from the chair she'd taken. "Where? Where are you going?"

"To arrest the killer," he said almost matter-of-factly.

"I'm going with you!" she insisted as she crossed the room to join him.

But he shook his head. "No, it's too dangerous. He's already tried to kill you too many times. You need to stay here."

"You're bringing deputies with you?" she asked. "You're not going alone."

He shook his head again and stepped out of the office. She rushed out after him, trailing him down the stairs to the lobby. "Hoge, he'll kill you, too!" She clutched at his arm, pulling him to a stop and around to face her. "He locked you in that trunk and in the vault. He doesn't care about you!"

Hoge flinched.

And she felt a pang of regret. But her fear was stronger. Her fear for him.

"Please, don't go alone," she implored him.

"I won't get close enough to arrest him if I don't go by myself," he said, then he tugged free of her grasp. At the exterior doors, he paused next to the security guard. "Hold her here until I drive away," he told him. "Then bring her back to the B and B."

"Hoge!" she called out, but he was already walking out of city hall, already heading toward his SUV.

The security guard stepped into her path, blocking the doorway, so that she didn't see the sheriff drive off. She just knew he was gone. She could have fought the older man. But she knew there was no fighting Hoge. He'd made up his mind. He was doing this alone— arresting his father.

She reached into her purse, and the security guard reached for his weapon, as if he expected her to draw one of her own. She didn't touch her can of pepper spray, though. She just pulled out her cell phone and punched in 9-1-1.

"What are you doing?" Bob asked. "Calling the cops on me? The sheriff just said—"

"Cold Creek police, what's your emergency?" Doreen asked, her voice emanating from the speaker of Eve's phone.

"The sheriff has gone off on his own to arrest a killer," Eve said.

"Ms. Collins?" Doreen asked. "What are you talking about? What killer?"

"The killer," she replied. "Ted Prentice."

Doreen's gasp rattled her cell speaker. "No…"

Bob's no echoed hers, and he staggered against the door. "I can't believe it…"

"It's true," she insisted. "I have DNA evidence…" That proved a familial relationship between the killer and Hoge and the mayor.

But she didn't have Ted Prentice's DNA. Would she get it? Or would he evade arrest again as he had for all these years?

"He needs to be apprehended," she said. "And I'm afraid the sheriff is going to get hurt if he tries to do it alone."

"Ted wouldn't hurt him," Doreen said. "He loves Hoge like his son."

Bob nodded. "That's true."

That was because Hoge was his son—the son he'd locked in a trunk, though. A son who could have died if not for the sheriff rescuing him in time.

"Ted tried to kill him before," she said. And she believed he'd have no qualms about doing it again.

The man was a monster.

A murderer…

"Hoge seems to know where he is," Eve said. "Where would that be?"

But even before Doreen answered, she'd realized where. They uttered the words together. "The cabin…"

"Send deputies there," Eve urged the dispatcher. "Tell them to hurry."

"I will," the woman replied. "But I really don't think the sheriff is in any danger."

Eve did. She had every reason not to trust Ted Prentice and so did Hoge. After all the killing he'd done, what was one more murder, even if that victim was his son?

Chapter Twenty-Two

Part of him had been holding out hope that he was wrong, that Eve Collins's DNA profiles were wrong. But she was too good. And he'd already been putting it together before she'd confirmed his suspicions.

When Hoge pulled into the clearing of the driveway near the cabin, he saw the vehicle already parked there—the truck with the crushed front bumper. The owner of that truck had driven Eve off the road; he'd tried to kill her.

Hoge knew who owned that truck. And he had no doubt that Eve was right. Ted—*Uncle Ted*—would probably try to kill him too. It was a risk he was willing to take for the answers he wanted, that he deserved. And he'd already waited too long for them. So he pushed open his door and stepped out on the gravel driveway.

His hand was on the butt of his gun sticking out of his holster, but he didn't have time to draw it before a gun cocked. A man stepped out of the shadows of the front porch, a shotgun in his hand—the double barrels aimed at Hoge.

The man was tall and broad—like Hoge. His head

was shaved. Hoge thought he'd done that because his hair had thinned like his brother's fine blond hair was thinning. But now he wondered if he'd done it so he didn't leave behind any DNA when he killed.

His eyebrows were dark, like Hoge's. His eyes were dark, too, like his soul.

Hoge's green eyes must have come from his mother. In the only photos he'd seen of her, from the crime scene, he hadn't been able to discern the color of her eyes. Just the shock and horror in them, what she must have felt when she'd stared into the face of her killer.

"I thought you left town," Hoge said. He couldn't believe that this was the same man he'd seen on the porch of the B and B just days ago, the man who'd squeezed his shoulder and offered him support and encouragement.

"I said I got called into work," Ted corrected him.

"Killing is your work?" Hoge asked. "You stayed to kill me?"

Ted snorted. "If I'd wanted you dead, kid, I would have killed you long ago."

"You nearly did," Hoge reminded him. "When you locked me in that trunk."

"You wouldn't shut up," Ted said, his mouth curling with disgust. "You just kept wailing and wailing." He shook his head. "I can't figure out why Rolland decided to keep you when nobody else would." He shrugged. "Pity, I guess."

"He loved me," Hoge said. That he would never doubt. Rolland Moore had made certain of that. No son could have been more loved than he had been.

Ted shrugged. "Your mama claimed the same nonsense. Wouldn't get an abortion like I told her to…then

kept threatening to tell everybody whose kid you were…"
He shuddered as if horrified that he'd fathered Hoge.

"Why would that have been so bad?" he asked. "Loretta was beautiful. Smart…"

"She was also too young when I was seeing her," Ted said. "I would have gone to jail for statutory rape. So I figured, might as well…"

Horror and pain overwhelmed Hoge, nearly making him bend forward—to absorb the blow of this man's—this monster's—confession. How had he never seen it before? The inhumanity…

"That's why you killed her?" Hoge asked. "To protect yourself. What about Amy? And Mary? And all the others…?"

Ted shrugged again. "Got away with it once. Then it just got to be kind of fun."

Hoge nearly shuddered with revulsion, but he didn't want to show Ted how much he was affecting him, how much he was disgusting him—because he suspected the man was having fun with him, just as he'd had fun killing…

"And the necklace?" Hoge asked. "Who's wearing it now?" Who had Ted marked for death next?

Ted kept his grasp on the shotgun with one hand while he dipped his other inside his sweater and pulled out the little peace symbol that hung from that thick, heavy chain.

"Your murder weapon…" Hoge murmured with repugnance and dread.

Ted dropped the necklace and put both hands back on the gun. "This will do too."

"How many?" he asked. "How many women did you kill?"

Ted shrugged as if he honestly didn't remember. Had there been so many that he'd forgotten?

The horror already gripping Hoge threatened to overwhelm him. He shared DNA with this man, this murderer. That was what he'd always feared…that his mother's killer had been his father, that half of his DNA came from a monster. But *Uncle* Ted? How had he never realized what kind of man Ted Prentice was?

"I don't understand…" Hoge murmured. "You've always seemed so nice. So normal…"

Ted chuckled. "I learned young how to act *acceptable*. But everyone's got a dark side, Hoge. Even you…"

Hoge shook his head in denial of Ted's words and of that fear that had haunted him, that had kept him from getting into a serious relationship with anyone. Because he hadn't trusted himself. He hadn't trusted that someday that darkness from which he'd come wouldn't overtake him and he'd hurt someone…someone he loved.

"Sure, you do," Ted said. "You like killing too."

"I've never hurt anybody," Hoge said. And he would make certain that he never did. He would keep his promise to himself to never get close to anyone, to never let anyone love him. He would make sure that after Ted's arrest, Eve returned to Pennsylvania. That she was safe and happy…without him in her life.

"You've killed fish, animals," Ted reminded him. "You're a hunter."

"For food," Hoge insisted. "Not for pleasure." He had never found pleasure in it, just the simple satisfaction of self-sufficiency.

"I've seen your face, boy," Ted said. "I've seen the pride. You like killing…just like me…"

"Is that why you're still here?" Hoge asked, pointing toward the gun. "You stuck around to kill me?"

"I'd rather kill that hot little consultant who came to town looking for me," Ted said.

"You tried," Hoge said.

He snorted. "She'd be dead if I really wanted her dead. No. I didn't touch her because I owe her old man. When the police questioned me about that secretary's murder nearly twenty years ago, I set him up to take the fall. Pete was a good guy—a lot like Rolland."

"Your name wasn't in the file," Hoge said, but he'd already figured out that he had been there. "Tom Wilson was."

"An alias," Ted said with a shrug. "I have a lot of them. That's why I like coming back here to Cold Creek. Reminds me who I really am."

"A killer…"

"You've got the genes for it too," Ted said. "Probably even my brother does."

A pang of panic struck Hoge. He'd left Eve alone with the mayor. But Bob was there too. The security guard wouldn't let anyone harm her.

"Have that little scientist explain genetics to you," Ted suggested. "I'm sure she's not going to touch you with a ten-foot pole now that she knows what you are, where you come from…"

Sirens wailed in the distance, and Hoge tensed as his father cursed.

"Should have known you wouldn't come alone," he murmured. "Still the scared little boy you always were. Too bad Rolland coddled you so much. That's why I hung around you two. I tried to make a man out of you."

He had been the first one to put a gun in Hoge's

hands, long before his father—his real father—had thought he was ready to hunt. But Ted had insisted, had said they'd started young too.

Hoge hadn't felt the pride that Ted claimed he had during that first hunting season. He'd felt guilt and pain and so much regret.

And the nightmares had returned…

Nightmares this man had caused.

But Ted had also joked around with him and slipped him his first beer and showed him magazines a young boy had had no business seeing…and so part of Hoge, that adolescent part of him, had thought Uncle Ted was cool. Now he understood that the man was actually *cold*—cold-blooded.

"Are you going to kill me?" he asked again as he pointed at the gun.

Just before the deputy's SUV made the turn onto the driveway leading to the cabin, the blast rang out. Birds fled from the trees, rising into the sky like a dark cloud. And a scream rose from Eve's throat, tearing free of it.

"Oh, no!"

They were too late, too late…

But she couldn't accept that. Couldn't accept that Hoge was gone. So she called on that faith her father encouraged her to have, and she prayed.

Please, God. Please, make sure that Hoge is okay. Please, protect him from the evil that's touched so much of his life. Please, God, save him. He's a good man.

She prayed the entire way down the long, twisty drive. She prayed that the man she loved had survived. He had to be alive.

"Miss, you need to stay here," the deputy told her

as he braked the SUV behind the sheriff's. His throat moved as he nervously swallowed before reaching for his door handle and his weapon at the same time.

But then Hoge came around his vehicle.

And another cry slipped through Eve's lips. One of relief and happiness. But when she jumped out of the vehicle, she saw the blood on him—spattered across his face and shoulders. "Are you hurt?" she asked.

He shook his head.

"The gun shot…" she murmured, then asked, "Did you…?"

He flinched. "No. I didn't kill him."

"Do we need an ambulance?" the deputy asked.

And Hoge shook his head again. "It's not necessary. He's gone."

"He got away?" Eve asked with alarm.

"No. I don't think he could face what he put your father through—imprisonment."

And so the killer had taken his last victim. Himself…

She had a horrible feeling that part of Hoge had died with him, though. He had loved this place, but Ted Prentice had ruined that for him, just as he'd ruined so much of Hoge's life.

"I'm sorry…" she murmured.

He shrugged. Then he swiped a hand over his face, smearing blood on his cheek. "Do you want to collect his DNA now or at the morgue?"

"What?"

"What do you need so that you can officially close all these cases and get out of Cold Creek?" he asked her, his voice as cold as the spray of the river running behind this cabin had been when it had struck her face.

She sucked in a breath, as if he'd struck her. "You want me gone?"

"It's for the best," he said. "Once you close these cold cases, there's nothing for you here. So you can leave as soon as possible."

Clearly he wanted her gone. Maybe she, not this place, was too painful a reminder of everything he'd learned about his past and about his real father.

Or maybe, like her ex-fiancé, Hoge had never really cared for her at all.

Her heart ached for him, for his pain and loss and for hers. But she forced herself to turn away from him and walk back toward the deputy's SUV.

It was all over now.

Not just her quest for justice but the quest she hadn't even realized she was on…

Her quest for love.

While she loved Hoge, he must not have loved her back, or he wouldn't be so anxious for her to leave.

Chapter Twenty-Three

Hoge couldn't help but wonder what might have been...

If his father hadn't framed hers for murder, if his father hadn't tried to kill her...

If Hoge had been Rolland Moore's biological son instead of the offspring of a monster...

She hadn't been able to trust him before she'd known that for certain. But now that she knew...

She probably couldn't wait to get out of town. But before the Collinses left, there was something Hoge had to do. So once he'd wrapped up with the coroner at the crime scene, he'd headed back to town.

He'd told the deputy to drive her back hours ago, so she might have already left. She had the justice she'd wanted, so she had no reason to stick around Cold Creek. Unless she intended to hold a press conference so that her father's name would fully and finally be cleared.

He couldn't blame her for wanting that, for wanting everyone to know that she wasn't a killer's child. So he wasn't surprised to find her father's car still parked in the lot next to the Queen Anne. Her father sat on the porch with Doreen, who jumped up when he approached.

"Are you all right?" she asked with concern. Her eyes were red and swollen; it was clear she'd been crying over him.

He didn't deserve her tears. "I'm fine," he said.

But she rushed down the steps and touched his face. "You have blood on you."

He did. He always would—because of who his father was. No wonder the James family had wanted nothing to do with him. He would have to tell them, though. He would have to tell all the victims' families that the murders had been solved. Unless Eve had already done it for him...

He glanced around but caught no sight of her. Maybe she was at the mayor's office holding that press conference, but he doubted that. Paul Prentice wouldn't want it known that he, too, was related to a killer.

If she was holding a press conference, it was on her own...

She wasn't the Collins Hoge wanted to talk to this time, though. Her father must have thought she was because he jumped up and offered, "I'll get Eve for you."

"Where is she?" he couldn't help but wonder.

"Sleeping," Doreen replied. "You shouldn't disturb her, Peter. She looked exhausted."

"I doubt she's sleeping," her father said.

But when he reached for the door, Hoge called out, "Don't get her. I don't want to talk to her." He couldn't... because he might be tempted to do something stupid, like ask her to stay, like ask her to find enough faith in him to trust him.

"Were you looking for me?" Doreen asked. "I have Cammie taking calls right now. I wouldn't have left the desk unattended."

"I know," he assured her. "I'd like to speak to Mr. Collins."

Doreen didn't move.

So he had to add, "Alone."

Her face flushed. "Yes, of course. I'm sorry…" And she started down the sidewalk.

"You can take the SUV," he told her.

"Are you sure?" she asked.

"Yeah, I'll walk back." If he went back…

He wasn't sure where he was going after this or what he was going to do. He just knew what he needed to do now. But he waited until Doreen drove off in his SUV before he turned back toward Mr. Collins.

The man was watching him, his blue eyes warm with compassion. "I'm sorry, son," he said, as he stepped forward and gripped Hoge's shoulder. "So very sorry…"

Tears stung Hoge's eyes. "That's what I came here to tell you…even though there's no apology that could ever make up for the ten years of your life that you lost."

"You didn't take those years from me," Bruce said. "You had nothing to do with that."

"But my father—"

Bruce shook his head. "That man was not your father. Your father was the man who raised you—the good, honorable man who raised you to be good and honorable too. That's why you're here—taking responsibility for something that had nothing to do with you—because you're like Rolland Moore. You're nothing at all like Ted Prentice."

"Eve told you," he surmised.

"I think I knew him as Tom Wilson," Bruce said.

"One of the last things he said was that he felt bad for framing you," Hoge admitted. "That's why he didn't kill Eve—just tried scaring her off instead. He felt he owed you."

Bruce sighed. "What a troubled man…"

"A monster," Hoge corrected him. "He was a monster. How can you have any compassion for him?"

"How can I not?" Bruce asked. "He will never know love like you and I have. He'll never give it, never receive it."

"I loved him," Hoge admitted. "I thought he was cool. I idolized a killer just like Eve accused me of doing. I'm not a good man like Rolland Moore, like you. I wish I was."

Bruce tightened his grip on Hoge's shoulder. "Don't. Don't let his darkness affect you. Don't let his betrayal make you not trust."

"I'll still trust other people," Hoge said. It was himself he couldn't trust now, his judgment, his genetics…

His words resonated within Eve. After everything he'd just learned, everything he'd been through, he could still trust? What was wrong with her that she couldn't? She pushed open the screen door through which she'd been eavesdropping and joined the two men on the porch. She loved them both.

She waited for that rush of fear she'd felt when she'd first acknowledged that she was falling for Hogan Moore. But she didn't feel it. She only felt warmth and happiness. Her father had been right about that, about the ability to give and receive love being a gift.

Feeling…even if it wound up in pain…was a gift.

"Then trust me," Eve told Hoge.

He stumbled back, away from her father, away from her. But before he could turn for the stairs, she caught his arm and held on to him. "Hoge…"

"Don't let him go," her father said. Then the screen door squeaked as he opened it. Before he retreated inside, he added, "Don't let each other go."

But the sheriff tugged his arm, trying to free it from her grasp. "You don't want me, Eve."

"I do," she said. Then she repeated something she'd said to him during one of their first meetings. "I need you. And now I mean it *like that*—exactly *like that*. I don't just need your help. I need you."

His breath shuddered out and his shoulders sagged. "How can you…after what you learned?"

"I learned you're an honorable man. That you're caring and honest and true and strong…and I love you," she said.

Hoge whirled around then. "Eve?"

"And I don't know if you feel the same way, but I have to tell you," she said. "I'm giving you my love and my trust."

He sucked in a breath before releasing it again in a ragged sigh. "I don't deserve it."

"Are you going to hurt me?" she asked. "Are you going to lie to me like my mother? Or cheat on me with my best friend like my ex-fiancé did?"

"Never," he said. "I would never purposely hurt you."

"You would never inadvertently hurt me either," she said. "You're too empathetic, too caring of other people—even people who've rejected and hurt you." She suspected now that Mr. James had always known who Hoge really was, that he was his grandson.

"But I'm the son of a killer," he said. "Of the man who framed your father for murder, who took him from you for ten years. How can you just forget about that?"

"I can't," she admitted. "But I can forgive." And she found that it was true and also freeing. She suddenly felt much lighter, her heart much warmer, than it ever had.

"You can forgive me?" he asked with wonder.

And she wondered how he could ask that.

"You don't need forgiveness," she said. "You've done nothing wrong. You are not responsible for the actions of your biological father. He's the one I'll forgive. And my mother and even my ex-fiancé and my friend…" Hanging on to her anger, her hurt, had only hurt her. She understood now what her father had been trying to tell her all along.

His lips curved up into a slight smile. "Eve, I don't understand how you can be so happy."

"It's because I can love," she said. "I can love and trust. You. Even if you don't return my feelings…"

He sighed, and his smile widened. "You know that I do," he said as he closed his strong arms around her and held her close to his heart. So close that she could feel its mad pounding. "I love you," he said. "I didn't want to admit it. I was worried I'd hurt you—"

She pressed her fingers over his lips. "You're not capable of purposely hurting someone. You're a good man, and finding you here was a blessing."

"But there's nothing here for you in Cold Creek."

"There's everything," she said. "You…" And he was everything to her now. "And I suspect my father is going to be staying for Doreen."

"But what about your career?" he asked. "All the important work you do?"

"I'll keep doing it," she said. "Maybe I'll set up my own lab here in Cold Creek."

"And if you have to travel, I'll go with you," he said. "I'll have the deputies handle things for a while so I can help you."

"Yes, with the two of us working cases, we'll solve them even faster."

He pulled back slightly but he didn't pull away. Instead he cupped her face in his palms and stared at her as if he couldn't believe what he was seeing.

Her love…

"Trust me," she said again.

"Always," he replied. "I was just thinking that we should probably call a press conference."

"To announce our love?" she asked.

"To announce that the cold cases have been solved, to make sure your father's name is cleared."

"He doesn't care," she said. She was the one who'd cared about that, but she cared even more about Hoge and she didn't want to hurt him.

"It's still the right thing to do," he insisted. "For all the victims."

"The mayor isn't going to like this press conference," she predicted. She also predicted he wouldn't be mayor for long. He wasn't strong enough to stay in Cold Creek with the stigma of having a killer in his family.

Hoge was, and she wasn't about to take him away from the town he'd sworn to serve and protect. They would figure it out, just as she'd promised.

Epilogue

They figured it out. First they got married, her father presiding over the ceremony before he began presiding over the town as the new mayor. He reminded everyone so much of their beloved former sheriff that he'd been elected in a landslide. Their more recent sheriff was even more beloved than the former one, though, because he took time to reach out to all the troubled teens.

Eve continued to use her expertise, and her husband's insights, to solve cold cases but no matter how often she had to travel, she always returned to Cold Creek. It was home now.

Wherever Hoge was, though, would have been home to her.

"You're back!" he exclaimed when she walked into his office after her latest trip. He jumped up from his chair and hugged her as if she'd been gone weeks instead of just a couple of days.

But in those couple of days, she'd learned something important. Something she needed to share with him.

"Case solved already?" he asked.

She nodded.

He brushed his mouth across hers before pulling back to study her face. "You're so beautiful. Even more than I remember...it's like you're glowing..."

She laughed. Once again her insightful husband had solved the case before she could reveal the conclusion to him. "I'm pregnant."

He let out an exultant shout and spun her around while she clutched at his strong shoulders. He quickly stopped and held her closely. "I didn't make you sick, did I?"

"No," she assured him. "I've been lucky. No morning sickness."

"You're not lucky," he said. "You're blessed. We both are."

They were. They truly were...

* * * * *

LOVE INSPIRED

Stories to uplift and inspire

Fall in love with Love Inspired—
inspirational and uplifting stories of faith
and hope. Find strength and comfort in
the bonds of friendship and community.
Revel in the warmth of possibility and the
promise of new beginnings.

Sign up for the Love Inspired newsletter
at **LoveInspired.com** to be the first
to find out about upcoming titles,
special promotions and exclusive content.

CONNECT WITH US AT:

 Facebook.com/LoveInspiredBooks

Twitter.com/LoveInspiredBks

Get 4 FREE REWARDS!

We'll send you 2 FREE Books plus 2 FREE Mystery Gifts.

Love Inspired Suspense books showcase how courage and optimism unite in stories of faith and love in the face of danger.

FREE
Value Over
$20

YES! Please send me 2 FREE Love Inspired Suspense novels and my 2 FREE mystery gifts (gifts are worth about $10 retail). After receiving them, if I don't wish to receive any more books, I can return the shipping statement marked "cancel." If I don't cancel, I will receive 6 brand-new novels every month and be billed just $5.24 each for the regular-print edition or $5.99 each for the larger-print edition in the U.S., or $5.74 each for the regular-print edition or $6.24 each for the larger-print edition in Canada. That's a savings of at least 13% off the cover price. It's quite a bargain! Shipping and handling is just 50¢ per book in the U.S. and $1.25 per book in Canada.* I understand that accepting the 2 free books and gifts places me under no obligation to buy anything. I can always return a shipment and cancel at any time. The free books and gifts are mine to keep no matter what I decide.

Choose one: ☐ **Love Inspired Suspense Regular-Print** (153/353 IDN GNWN) ☐ **Love Inspired Suspense Larger-Print** (107/307 IDN GNWN)

Name (please print)

Address   Apt. #

City.   State/Province   Zip/Postal Code

Email: Please check this box ☐ if you would like to receive newsletters and promotional emails from Harlequin Enterprises ULC and its affiliates. You can unsubscribe anytime.

Mail to the **Harlequin Reader Service:**
IN U.S.A.: P.O. Box 1341, Buffalo, NY 14240-8531
IN CANADA: P.O. Box 603, Fort Erie, Ontario L2A 5X3

Want to try 2 free books from another series! Call 1-800-873-8635 or visit www.ReaderService.com.

---

*Terms and prices subject to change without notice. Prices do not include sales taxes, which will be charged (if applicable) based on your state or country of residence. Canadian residents will be charged applicable taxes. Offer not valid in Quebec. This offer is limited to one order per household. Books received may not be as shown. Not valid for current subscribers to Love Inspired Suspense books. All orders subject to approval. Credit or debit balances in a customer's account(s) may be offset by any other outstanding balance owed by or to the customer. Please allow 4 to 6 weeks for delivery. Offer available while quantities last.

Your Privacy—Your information is being collected by Harlequin Enterprises ULC, operating as Harlequin Reader Service. For a complete summary of the information we collect, how we use this information and to whom it is disclosed, please visit our privacy notice located at corporate.harlequin.com/privacy-notice. From time to time we may also exchange your personal information with reputable third parties. If you wish to opt out of this sharing of your personal information, please visit readerservice.com/consumerschoice or call 1-800-873-8635. **Notice to California Residents**—Under California law, you have specific rights to control and access your data. For more information on these rights and how to exercise them, visit corporate.harlequin.com/california-privacy.

LIS21R2

SPECIAL EXCERPT FROM

LOVE INSPIRED SUSPENSE
INSPIRATIONAL ROMANCE

Searching for her best friend's remains could help forensic anthropologist Melanie Hutton regain her memories of when they were both kidnapped—and put her right back in the killer's sights. But can Detective Jason Cooper set the past aside to help her solve his sister's murder...and shield Melanie from the same fate?

Read on for a sneak peek at
Buried Cold Case Secrets,
a new Love Inspired Suspense story by Sami A. Abrams!

Melanie wiped her hand down her face. "Jason. We're going to be working together for the foreseeable future. Do you think we can call a truce at least while we do our jobs?"

His jaw twitched, and he remained silent.

She'd asked a lot, but the strain between them had to stop. She watched him for a few minutes then shook her head.

"Never mind." She pushed from the trunk and limped to the hole in the ground. Her lead-filled heart threatened to drop to her feet. To think that fifteen years ago she'd had a crush on him. If only she could return to those carefree days. The days before she had died on the inside and her friend had died for real.

Someday, Allison, I'll find your body. I promise.

She swiped the wetness from her cheeks and lowered herself into the grave. The movement mimicked her mood. She picked up her trowel and searched for more bones.

An hour later, Melanie's headache had become unbearable, causing her stomach to roil. Scanning the grave, she spotted the paintbrush she used for delicate work. She grasped the handle but dropped it. She tried again, but her fingers refused to cooperate. Her eyelids grew heavy. Something was off. She sat on the edge of the hole.

"Jason, help." Her words were slurred. She struggled to stay upright. The trees in front of her blurred and swayed.

He kneeled down and came face-to-face with her. "What's wrong?"

"I don't know."

"Help me out here. What's the last thing you did?"

"I—I…" She struggled against the gray cloud jumbling her thoughts. "Took a break a while ago. Only digging since."

His gaze flew to a spot behind her.

She wilted into him. Her vision tunneled, and darkness closed in.

"Keith! Grab the cooler and her bag!"

Jason's frantic voice registered, but her body had shut down.

His warm arms lifted her.

Her cheek bounced against his chest in cadence with the pounding of his feet on the path.

His rhythmic breathing was the last thing she heard before the world went dark.

Don't miss
Buried Cold Case Secrets *by Sami A. Abrams,*
available January 2022 wherever
Love Inspired Suspense books and ebooks are sold.

LoveInspired.com

IF YOU ENJOYED THIS BOOK
WE THINK YOU WILL ALSO LOVE

LOVE INSPIRED
INSPIRATIONAL ROMANCE
MOUNTAIN RESCUE

Courage. Danger. Faith.

Find strength and determination in stories
of faith and love in the face of danger.

AVAILABLE JANUARY 25, 2022